Publisher:
John Betancourt

Editor:
Robert M. Price

Managing Editor:
Sean Wallace

Distribution Manager:
Abner Gibber

Strange Tales is published quarterly by Wildside Press LLC, 9710 Traville Gateway Drive #234, Rockville MD 20850. Postmaster & others: send change of address and other subscription matters to Wildside Press, attn: *Strange Tales*, 9710 Traville Gateway Drive #234, Rockville MD 20850. Single copies: $7.50 (magazine edition), postage included in the U.S.A. Add $2.00 per copy for shipping elsewhere. Subscriptions: 4 issues for $19.95 in the U.S.A. and its possessions, $29.95 in Canada, and $39.95 elsewhere. All payments must be in U.S. funds and drawn on a U.S. financial institution. If you wish to use PayPal to pay for your subscription, email your payment to: wildside@sff.net.

Tell us what you think!
Reach *Strange Tales* online
by email at:

strange@wildsidepress.com

Fiction and poetry submissions: Authors may submit work to the editor. Please query first to insure that the editor is currently reading new submsisions. Queries to: criticus@aol.com..

Art submissions: Please email art@wildsidepress.com.

STRANGE TALES OF MYSTERY AND TERROR   **VOL. 4, NO. 3**

Contents

4

THE BELFRY

by Robert M. Price

Recently I had the honor of appearing, along with my beloved friend and colleague S.T. Joshi, at the Cthulhu One convention in Madison, Wisconsin. As always in such events, it was great fun touring the dealers room to see what blasphemous books and terror-trinkets the eldritch craftsmen might have to offer. I was tempted to purchase *yet another* sculpture of Great Cthulhu, an artist's conception of the totemic idol featured in Lovecraft's "The Call of Cthulhu." But I realized I didn't have any more space to put the thing! Besides, I already had more than enough Cthulhu effigies anyway. So I contented myself with a smaller Cthulhu bust, a fine, thumb-size depiction of "the awful squid head."

The highlight of the trip was an unscheduled visit I made, with Joshi and his wife Leslie, along with other acolytes, out to nearby Sauk City, the home of August W. Derleth and Arkham House. Because of these associations, Sauk City itself has nearly the same mythic resonances as Arkham or Dunwich! I had never visited the place before, a surprising fact even to me, in view of the many years of my Lovecraftian obsession.

Our first stop was the Sauk City cemetery, where Derleth's remains tarry—unless Pickman got farther west than anyone thought! The grave, almost directly across from "Place of Hawks," Derleth's home and the Arkham House warehouse, is a lot easier to locate than the grave of Lovecraft in Swan Point Cemetery in Providence, Rhode Island. And I doubt very much that any

weird fiction devotees had ever been chased away in the midst of holding esoteric rites at Derleth's grave, as has happened at Lovecraft's. And yet, while my friends chatted pleasantly, I must confess to a surprising moment of sepulchral mystical communion.

As I stood by the grave of August Derleth that May Eve, resting my hand on the marble stone, I could not help addressing a few silent words to whatever figurative presence of Derleth might yet lurk there. "I never met you, but I am your successor. I have taken up the banner from your failing hands." Not directly, of course, but at a distance of one remove. Everyone in our field knows full well that Lin Carter was the immediate successor of August Derleth as both theoretician of the Cthulhu Mythos and as editor and anthologist in the Lovecraftian genre. In Lin's memoir "A Day in Derleth Country," he mentioned how Derleth had sold him a pair of original Clark Ashton Smith sculpted bookends, the "Treasure Guardians," one of them Smith's own representation of his deity Tsathoggua. To me that symbolized the passing of the torch, which Lin indefatigably held high once Derleth passed from the scene in 1971.

Upon Lin Carter's death in 1988, both the Treasure Guardians and the legacy they represented passed on to me. Lin and I had worked together on projects including my magazine *Crypt of Cthulhu*, just as Lin had worked with Augie on *The Arkham Sampler* and on his own book *Lovecraft: A Look behind the "Cthulhu Mythos."* Under the auspices of Chaosium, Inc., I was able to carry to comple-

tion various projects Lin had wanted to publish. I have ventured to carry on the literary adventures of Thongor of Lemuria. And now, of course, as editor of the revived *Strange Tales of Mystery and Terror,* I am proud to follow in Lin's footsteps again. I know he would have enjoyed the various yarns that grace our pages this time out. He'd surely have loved "Blood of the Moon God," by British fantasy master Adrian Cole. It is a new adventure of Henry Kuttner's sword and sorcery hero Elak of Atlantis, and Lin considered Kuttner actually the superior of Robert E. Howard. (All right, someone out there will object

that Elak's original adventures appeared in *Weird Tales,* not *Strange Tales,* but I'm not that picky!).

Who will take possession of the Treasure Guardians next? Who knows? Maybe the shade of Lin Carter, August Derleth, or even of Smith himself will miss them and come for them late one moonless night! But their legacy lives on through all of us, the writers and readers of *Strange Tales.*

—Robert M. Price
Hierophant of the Horde

WILDSIDE PRESS ORDER FORM

QUANTITY	TITLE	PRICE
	SUBTOTAL	
In MD? Please add 5% State Sales Tax		
U.S. Shipping & Handling: $3.95 for 1-2 books, $1 per additional book.		
TOTAL		

Enclosed is payment of $_____ by ☐ check ☐ money order ☐ Visa ☐ MasterCard ☐ American Express.

NAME:_____

ADDRESS:_____

ADDRESS:_____

or order online at <www.wildsidepress.com>

CC# _____-_____-_____-_____

EXP:____/____ Signature:_____

Mail to: Wildside Press LLC
9710 Traville Gateway Dr. #234
Rockville MD 20850

Use this form, a photocopy, or write out your order on a separate paper.

BLOOD OF THE MOON GOD

by Adrian Cole

illustrated by David Grilla

Chapter One: Treachery by Moonlight

"By Ishtar!" growled the short, thick-set figure, sweat gleaming on his puffed-out cheeks in the moonlight. "I swear for every one of those scum we cut down, a dozen more rise up from the night." His blade hissed in the air in a warning pass, dripping with the blood of those he had killed during the frantic skirmish in these hills.

"Save your breath, Lycon," said the tall, thin warrior beside him, his own blade, a slim rapier, also gleaming with recently spilled blood. "They have withdrawn, if only for a moment."

"Sire," came a third voice from the night-shadows beside him, "we are surrounded! I fear they are gathering in even greater numbers." He indicated the lower slopes, where, among the stunted tress, scores of armed men formed a circling shield wall, forcing the king and his small party further up the exposed face of the hill. Far below, at the distant edge of the sea, the night lamps of the city of Epharra winked and ships rode silently at anchor, oblivious of the plight of their ruler.

"Let them come!" snarled Lycon. "This is as good a place as any to die. Though I'd rather it had been with a jug or two of good wine inside me!"

"Aye, and with another in your free hand!" laughed Elak, though there was little humour in his grim tone. "This was a trap and I was a fool to slip into it so easily. The kingship has made a soft, pampered target of me. There was a time when I'd have had wit enough to evade such pitfalls."

Lycon grunted, his remarkably simian face studying the sprawl of those who had fallen, two score or more of the heaped bodies draped across rock and heather, sightless eyes gazing up at the skies in death. "Even so, your sword arm doesn't lack for speed or effectiveness."

Elak turned to the sergeant at arms beside him and the last handful of his own soldiers who had so far survived the assault in the forest. "Who are they, Granthos? Do you recognise them?"

The ambushers had appeared like ghosts, evidently sent here by their master to one end: to bring down the king and his protectors. But it was no secret in the palace that Elak liked to ride at night, to relieve himself of the trials and tribulations of ruling his empire in Cyrena, a mantle which he had reluctantly taken upon himself a year before, after the murder of his brother, Orander and the defeat of the alien, Karkora. Any number of his enemies could have set this up. Treason yet festered like a sore in these lands.

"Hired cut-throats, sire. Mercenaries, pirates, the vermin of the wharfs and alleys of Epharra. But my money would be on Scuvular, your cousin, being behind this. 'Tis said that he covets your crown. He's enough riches to hire such a rabble."

"Scuvular!" snorted Lycon derisively. "That gross maggot! He runs half the pirate fleets this side of Atlantis. I warned you to drag him out of his city council lair, Elak!"

Elak grinned, his face like a wolf's mask in the glow of the huge moon. "You did indeed, Lycon. But he hides his dealings with consummate skill. I could not touch him without proof."

"Pah! A few minutes alone with me and this—" he brandished his blade, "and he'd soon blabber the truth!"

"I'm the king, Lycon. I have to use more diplomatic methods these days."

The clinking of armour down in the trees cut short the discussion, for the pursuers were preparing to launch a final assault. Elak and his small company were been pinned here. There were rocks behind them and they made their way upwards. A semi-circle of armed men came out of the trees after them like hunting wolves, swords gleaming. Their purpose was clear: they meant to kill every last man of the fleeing party.

Granthos sent a dozen warriors into a narrow defile between two immense shoulders of rock and gestured for Elak and Lycon to follow before bringing up the rear himself with the last of the royal guard. Neither the king nor Lycon liked having to be sheltered by the men and would have preferred to be in the forefront of any fighting, but Elak forced himself to accept the protocols of kingship. He twisted in the narrow confines between the rocks as he heard the renewed clash of steel behind him, where Granthos and his men were holding back the rabble assault.

As Elak wormed his way after the vanguard, face passing close to the naked stone walls, he saw by the moonlight that they were etched with pictographs and unfamiliar glyphs. There was no time to study them, but something in those weird designs made the hackles on the back of his neck rise. Lycon had seen them, too, and he cursed under his breath.

"What is this place?" he growled. "It reeks of ancient sorcery."

"There are tales about these hills," said Elak. "That's why they're usually shunned. Old gods, lost races. Relics from before the dawn of our time."

"Let's hope it's all talk," said Lycos.

They emerged into a rough circle of huge rocks; it was as though the top of the hill had been ripped open, a deep hollow formed at its crest. This was empty, grassed over, mostly in shadow, for the surrounding rocks and boulders rose up in a tall, enclosing wall. In the pallid light, the boulders assumed the shapes of enormous hunched figures, like oversized demi-gods, their stone faces squinting down into the hollow at the rude intrusion of the humans.

Elak's attention was diverted to the cleft in the rocks behind him as Granthos and the last of his men spilled through. They blocked the mouth of the passage with their shields, indicating that it would not be long before the pursuit emerged.

"We can hold them all night, sire!" Granthos avowed. "But in such a remote place as this, we could be holed up for days. You'll be missed in the palace, sire, and searched for, but the enemy has chosen this place cunningly."

Elak was studying the surrounding wall. Moonlight gleamed upon it, making it look slick and treacherous. It would be difficult to scale its face. The only practical way out was the way they had entered. He cursed himself for being fool enough to put them all at such a disadvantage. But there was no time for further deliberation, for the enemy was upon them. Swords clashed in the darkness as Granthos' men held the entrance. Elak and Lycos made to support them from the rear, eager to be involved, hating inactivity.

Whoever goaded the enemy forces onward was ruthless in their approach, forcing them on, careless of the crush. Men fell and were trampled by their own companions as the great weight of bodies behind them heaved and thrust. Granthos and his men hacked and cut at their opponents, downing dozens of them, partially choking the entrance, but more and more of the enemy clambered over the fallen, hurling themselves forward with a mad abandon, as though possessed. Elak suspected sorcery, guessing supernatural forces had animated the warriors, whose wild faces suggested a kind of madness. Scuvular was reputed to be ruthless in his pursuit of power.

With a last burst of determination, a dozen of the assailants broke past Granthos and his soldiers, howling with triumph, blades and pikes ripping into the defenders. Elak, Lycon and the others were forced back into the center of the hollow, the ground under their feet seeming to drum as the melee grew more violent. Instinctively the defenders formed themselves into a circle, steel clashing, sparks flying, the air thick with ozone, the walls ringing with the howls of the assailants and the shrieks and screams of the wounded and dying, for it had become a bloody affray.

Lycon fought like a caged tiger, belying his portliness, while beside him Elak cut and thrust with deadly speed and skill, hacking down the enemy like so many stalks of wheat. A bizarre smile played on his lips, as though even here, in this deadly trap, he burned with a fierce pleasure at the battle, balanced on the brink of death at every stroke. For all this, the defenders were pressed back into the center of the hollow, picked off one by one by the sheer tenacity of their opponents. A rising maniacal fury seemed to blaze in the eyes of the assailants, who were careless of the blades that cut into them. It took a dozen strikes to fell them, where usually one good thrust would have gutted them.

Elak felt something underfoot give: the ground had heaved like the flank of a huge beast. Lycon had felt it, too, staggering to one side. But before they could comment on it there came a deafening rumble, as if thunder echoed below them. The ground shook once more, then cracked and crumbled as if it were no more than a thin crust: dust blew upwards and men shrieked in horror.

Elak felt himself plummet into sudden darkness and in the next few fleeting seconds realised that the center of the hollow had completely given way, plunging him, Lycon and the last of his men down into the depths below the hill. Around them, their enemies fell, too. There was no time to pray to their primitive gods. Seconds later they were enveloped in the icy embrace of black waters. The cold grip shook Elak as a dog shakes a rat and his head burst the surface, where he dragged in a lungfull of air and howled at the moon high in the orifice overhead.

Instinctively, sword gripped in his teeth, Elak stroked

out across the surface, assuming this was a pool with sides. He had to get out of the freezing waters as quickly as possible, or succumb to their deadly cold. Lycon grunted beside him, alternatively swearing and choking but somehow keeping afloat.

The drab moonlight faintly illuminated a bizarre scene behind them. Elak's warriors had done as their leader and were stroking for the shore. But those who had attacked them seemed hell-bent on following up their attack, swinging their weapons, shrieking like demons, making no effort to get ashore. One by one they sank into the black waters, never to rise up again. Whatever demented force drove them denied them a choice of actions. Unable to swim, they thrashed about like huge, gaffed fish, ironically pulled down to their doom.

Exhausted and shivering, Elak, Lycon and the last of their companions, heaved themselves up on the be-slimed shore of the pool. By the overhead moonlight they could see the pool was some hundred feet across, perfectly circular, like a huge well. Slowly the waters stilled and the last ripples washed ashore. Every one of their assailants had been dragged down below the surface.

"By the Nine Hells!" called Lycon, pointing. "We have scotched one snake only to face another."

Elak turned. The darkness around the walls of the cavern gleamed with a sickly green glow and by this he could discern more shapes, hunched beings half the size of a man. Many of them held aloft gnarled staffs, from which the green glow spread. And in that ghastly light, a throng of the creatures gazed upon the intruders from huge eyes that had never seen the light of the outer air. Elak and his company had stumbled into a region of nightmare from beyond the reach of time.

Chapter Two: Shadow of the Serpent

Teeth chattering, Lycon made ready to cut loose among the hideous half-men that pressed forward from the confines of the cavern. Their skin was like the skin of fish, squamous and with a green tint, the sides of their thick faces lined with a row of tiny gills. But as they saw Lycon raise his weapon, they drew back, their combined voices croaking with fear in the semi-dark. They were more toad-like than like men.

"Put up your weapons," came a voice, and a moment later another figure emerged from the back of the cavern.

BY ADRIAN COLE 11

With a shock, Elak recognised the cloaked druid at once, the face within the enfolding hood.

"Dalan! By Ishtar! Is it you? How do you come to be in such a place?"

The druid, for it was indeed he, came further forward, an enigmatic smile on his lips. Beside him, the weird under-folk drew back, clearly in respect of him. "I have been waiting for you. I knew that Scuvular intended to snare you. You must forgive the methods I employed to rescue you, but my choices were limited."

"Curse it, Dalan!" growled Lycon. "Did you have to have us immolated in ice!"

"I knew you'd survive it. Especially you, Lycon."

Lycon swore crudely at the reference to his girth, but in truth he was hugely relieved to see the druid.

"And I knew Scuvular's vermin would perish in the water," Dalan added.

"I trust you know a comfortable way out of this pit and back to the surface world," said Elak, sheathing his sword. It was clear now that the strange beings around them meant no harm.

"I do," nodded Dalan. "But I fear that there is work to be done in this unsavoury realm before you can return to your kingdom, Elak. Or should I call you Zeulas?"

"At court, men call me by my true name. But when I'm away from the rigours of the palace, I still use my assumed name."

"You were always reluctant to take the throne," said Dalan grimly. "Though it is yours by birthright."

"Aye. But I'll trade a night of mayhem such as this for a month among the cushions and simpering ladies of court!"

"Then you'll warm to the work we have here."

Lycon wiped his lips. "Perhaps we could get dried out first! These waters would freeze the hide off a walrus. And I don't suppose your army of frogs have such a thing as a bottle of wine hidden away in these passages?"

"Possibly."

"Who are they?" asked Elak, aware that the creatures had remained almost completely silent through the exchanges. "In some ways they remind me of the Children of Dagon. And yet they are not hostile."

"They are related," nodded the druid. "They are the Aquarri, sea dwellers, an ancient race that flourished in Atlantis long before the first men struggled up from its mires. They are peace loving sea farmers and they have suffered near extinction at the hands of several other species. Including the Children of Dagon. Now their shrinking kingdom has been invaded once more. They need our help."

"Invaded!" repeated Lycon. "By whom? The ac-cursed Northmen again? By Ishtar, I've seen enough Vikings to last me a dozen lifetimes!"

"Would it were them," said Dalan. "Come, I will show you."

He led the company out of the cavern and down a series of tunnels, cut from the living rock, and in the strange glow of the torches, Elak and his companions felt themselves warmed, the chills of the pool losing their grip on their bones. The Aquarri followed them, still silent, their huge, sad eyes watching, like obedient hounds awaiting a master's command.

Elak noticed again the carvings on the walls, which spoke of events and a time long past. He recognised the toad-like men among the depictions, many of which seemed to involve religious practices of some kind, obeisance to aquatic gods that were hinted at but not shown. Gods of the deep waters.

"We are nearing their village," said Dalan, pointing to a crossroads in the tunnel ahead. But his face clouded and he urged everyone to flatten themselves up against the cave sides. Instantly the lights were extinguished, plunging the whole run into utter darkness. Lycon felt his heart thumping in his chest. Suddenly the immense weight of the stone above him seemed to press down, about to pulp him where he stood.

But there was a faint glow——up ahead. The crossroads shimmered as another torch seemed to be approaching it from the intersecting path. Dalan had murmured something, a druidic chant, and it hung like a shielding cloak over Elak and the company. They could hear the approach of another being. A shadow fell across the crossroads, long and broad.

Elak saw the figure emerge. It stood, fully seven feet tall, limned in the glow of the sputtering torch it carried. It was a warrior, decked in light armour, a sword and dagger at its belt, a wide helm across its brow. On its broad chest, emblazoned on the thin metal there was an emblem, a lurid aquatic creature only half seen in this light. And although the being stood erect and turned its eyes this way and that in the manner of a human, searching the shadows of the tunnels, it was no man. For Elak saw the long, thick tail, the snout and features.

Dressed in the trappings of a human warrior, it was nevertheless *a creature with the head of a huge serpent.*

Chapter Three: From the Dawn of Time

The serpent man's forked tongue flicked out, tasting the air of the tunnels, seeking its prey: its lidded eyes scanned every crevice so that Elak was certain of being discovered. But Dalan's spell held and at last the beast seemed satisfied that no one was there and moved on down the cross tunnel and out of sight.

"By the Nine Hells, what *was* it?" whispered Lycon at his elbow.

"Thought to be long extinct," said the druid softly. "They ruled Atlantis and Valusia long before men. They were wiped out over the centuries. But as you saw, some survived."

He said no more for the moment, anxious to get the company down the tunnels to the enclave of the Aquarri. This proved to be little more than a series of complex caves, half of which ran deep under water in another huge chamber. On the far side of this, the wall had been breached by the underground waters; a wide tunnel wormed its way far under the continent, to the open sea itself, Dalan told them.

"They have had to hide far from the eyes of men. That or perish. So, too, with the serpent men. But they tire of the dark places. They yearn to go back to the surface and live upon it and in its jungles."

"How many of them are there?" said Elak.

Dalan shook his head. "Far more than we could have dreamed. They are preparing for war. The time of their god is close at hand."

"Their god?" said Elak.

"The Moon God, Saaraaza. They give blood sacrifices to him. Human blood. And in their workings there is some terrible purpose. These humble creatures have warned me of it, though what its true extent is, I have yet to learn. Only that it presages a dire peril for all of Atlantis."

"You have a plan to thwart them?" said Elak with a grin.

Dalan's own features were clouded. "We need to know more before we act."

Lycon muttered something. "Why not just get us back to Cyrena, where we can gather a force, return and wipe out this nest of serpents?"

"I see you still do not count subtlety among your virtues, Lycon. No, we would only send the serpent men deeper into hiding. We need to draw them out and remove their head."

"How?" said Elak.

"They have certain unnatural skills. I have watched them secretly. They are able to shape-shift. They can take on the guise of a man. The old legends say that they almost won Valusia itself by use of metamorphosis. You must be wary of those you deal with. Here—wear these amulets. They will both protect and forewarn you of treachery." Dalan passed them both a thin amulet, curled like a golden serpent.

"We will play them at their own game," Dalan grinned mirthlessly.

Lycon scowled suspiciously. "What do you mean?"

"There are spells that I can weave about us. To metamorphose *us*."

Lycon swore. "If you think I'm going to turn into a filthy serpent—"

Elak chuckled in the gloom. "It can't be worse than the state you get into after one of your all night binges, my friend! But if it works—it would be a perfect way to deceive them."

Lycon was evidently not convinced. He held up his arm, the bracelet gleaming. "Do they not have these? Are they not able to detect perfidy themselves?"

Dalan shrugged. "Of course, I cannot be certain. But it is unlikely. They are, I suspect, far too arrogant to anticipate an enemy using their own deceits against them."

"Then I'm for it!" said Elak. "Come, druid, do your worst!"

"Soon," replied Dalan. "There is a conclave. Shortly after daybreak."

They rested for a few hours in a low cave set aside from the homes of the Aquarri, breakfasting on dried fish and stale bread that Dalan had brought with him from the surface. The druid told them more of the serpent men and their history. "Over the centuries, Atlantis has been slowly sinking. A combination of events both natural and unnatural have contributed to this. The earth is shifting, its continents rising and falling over the epochs. And in the endless wars between species, colossal powers have been invoked, mad gods have torn loose from their chains, sorcery has riven the skies and thrown the oceans into turmoil. You met the Children of Dagon and know well enough what they sought to achieve."

"Aye," Lycon grimaced. "The sinking of the empire."

"Is that what these serpent creatures desire?" Elak asked.

"They are not amphibious and their gods are not found under the ocean. But they will use whatever powers they can in an attempt to restore what once they had. Prior to the golden age of Atlantis and Valusia, when the kings of men ruled over the primordial world, it was the time of the serpent men. They grew up out of the age of reptiles, their power and control absolute. Who knows what sorceries and blackest magics they wielded? But there are ancient records, once held in prediluvian vaults, that speak of wars among them, dreadful conflicts that ripped and tore the world asunder, weakening the power of the serpents.

Their own lusts undid them, for in the wake of these dreadful wars, Man rose from the mire and established his first kingdoms.

"These centred on Atlantis, Valusia and Mu. The serpent empire waned over centuries of conflict as Man spread across the world. Gradually the new masters took control and the serpent men slid down towards extinction. But Man's empires have almost succumbed to the same fate as his predecessors! New empires rise. Sorcery and wild magic again rend the skies. Men return to Atlantis, not to trade with her, but to assail her. You have tasted such turmoil, Elak. The Vikings would ravish your empire and raise up their own gods here."

"Aye," nodded the king. "We've not seen the last of them."

"The world is in upheaval. The serpent men know this. They will use the wars of men to their own ends."

"Divide and conquer. An old strategy, but an effective one."

"It begins here. Come," said Dalan, getting to his feet. "They meet soon."

Chapter Four: Voice of the Traitor

Three hunched figures moved cautiously along the narrow ledge, high in the vaulted cavern. By the dim glow of cressets set both above and below them, they could see that the ledge led around the rocky terrain towards a strange citadel, hewn out of the naked rock of the cave system. Unlike the modest works of the Aquarri, this was complex, a small city, its squat buildings rising tier upon tier into the torch-lit shadows high above the waters at its base. Several such ledges bisected the cliff face, all leading to the citadel. It was clearly the home of the serpent men.

The trio of shapes moved further down the ledge, their heads covered in wide hoods, the last of them pausing to curse roundly, profaning the gods of Atlantis.

"Hurry, Lycon!" hissed the leader. "The sooner the city embraces us, the sooner we can hide ourselves from prying eyes."

It was Dalan who had spoken, though Lycon still grimaced at sight of him, for he had exercised the promised sorcery and metamorphosed into a serpent man, the snout of his elongated head just visible in his hood. Lycon shuddered: in his own guise as a serpent being he felt somehow unclean, as if he had been dipped in something repellent.

Beside him, Elak's snort of amusement came out as a sharp hiss. "When this is over, my friend, I'll be glad to join you in as many goblets of wine as you can drink!"

"Aye, let us bathe in it! And I'll warrant that any subsequent visions and distortions of reality will be as nothing to this sorry state of affairs!"

Dalan hissed at them to be silent and they acceded, slouching along behind him in the gloom. A short while later they entered the citadel through a low portal that led along a sinewy tunnel, a true serpent's lair. There were no guards, for the serpent men had no cause to think themselves in danger of discovery down here in the guts of the earth. The place was a maze, but Dalan seemed to know his way about: Elak realised the druid must have been here several times, risking much to learn the workings of the enemy.

Just as Elak thought he would suffocate in the sepulchral confines of the tunnels, they came out on to another ledge, a balcony with a low parapet, lit vaguely from above by another of the cressets. Peering over the parapet, the three figures could see down into a semicircular area where a score or more of the serpent men had gathered. Most were seated, while around the perimeter others stood stiffly, holding curved pikes, watching over the conclave. In the stillness, the voices from below drifted up clearly, though at first Elak and Lycon found it impossible to understand the hissing speech of the serpent beings.

Dalan, however, translated the gist of it. "As I told you, they are to invoke their Moon God, Saaraaza. They have an ally. See!"

Elak studied the shadows below and watched now as someone emerged from another low portal into the arena. This was no serpent man but *a man of his own race!* And as the man spoke, Elak recognised the voice only too well.

"Scuvular!" snorted Lycon. "By Ishtar, that traitorous scum——!"

They waited, all three of them outraged, keeping silent with difficulty.

"Prince of Atlantis," came the voice of the most prominent of the serpent men. "The time of your elevation grows near. Are your own servants prepared for their part in the conquest?"

Scuvular wore a rich, purple robe, his corpulent shape limned in the torchlight, cold eyes gleaming from a fat, pasty face. "Indeed they are, Quarrass-Theen."

"And the king? You have eliminated him?"

Scuvular's dark brows knitted in a deep scowl. "Not yet, Lord of Serpents, but my servants have him penned up in the very hills above you. I will deliver his head to you ere long. And those of his closest confidantes."

"Tonight," came the chilling voice of the huge serpent man Scuvular had addressed, "it will be the Moon of Saaraaza. At its zenith in the heavens, its rays will fall upon the holy idol in the citadel. The blood of our enemies will flow and the lost powers of the millennia will awaken. Before them, the cities of Men will perish!"

"And the palace of the king will drop into my hand like a ripened fruit."

"A fitting reward for your part in this conquest, Scuvular, who shall be the last king of men in Atlantis."

"Only as your servant, great Quarrass-Theen." And Scuvular bowed low, his head almost to the ground.

Lycon could scarcely contain his fury. "Had I a bow," he muttered, but Elak gripped his arm.

"This is not the time," whispered the king. "Dalan, what does the serpent mean? What powers are to be unleashed?"

Dalan shook his head. "Evil sorcery, but that's all I know. Under its flow, the serpent army will rise. They think that, with Elak removed, Atlantis will be in disarray."

"Then," said Elak, "we must disrupt this ceremony. Can you lead us to the citadel and the idol they spoke of? If it is a key part of the ritual, we must destroy it."

Lycon spat another curse. "Sounds like a good plan to me."

They left the balcony, going back into the gloom of the tunnels, but they had gone but a few paces within when they heard the telltale clink of swords being drawn. Out of the darkness a dozen serpent warriors stepped.

"What are you doing here?" hissed the first of them.

Dalan bowed. "Returning to our quarters, having completed our guard duty."

"You lie!" snapped the warrior, sword flicking forward, its edge cutting the air an inch from Dalan's serpent features.

For answer, Elak drew his own blade and lunged with it, its point sinking deep into the throat of the serpent man. It gurgled, blood running from the fatal wound, and dropped to its knees, groping uselessly at the air. Elak kicked it aside and chopped at another of the serpent men. Within moments a frightful contest ensued. Lycon, hampered by the cloak and the heavy build of the shape he had adopted, found himself driven back to the wall. "By the Nine Hells, can't we have done with the disguise and fight as men fight!" he yelled at Dalan.

"Hold!" came a sharp command from beyond the pressing serpent guards. As one they drew back, sword points held before them, ringing the three men. From between the serpent ranks, a figure came forward, dressed in a rich, purple robe. Elak saw, with a sinking heart, that it was Scuvular himself.

"Well, well," said the traitor. "Serpent men fighting serpent men? That has a ring of falsity to it." He pointed at the amulet on Dalan's wrist. "Remove that, before I have your hand cut from you."

Slowly the druid did as bidden. And as the amulet fell to the stone floor, Dalan was revealed in his natural form.

Scuvular nodded. "The druid! Faithful as a dog. And as for these two, why, they can only be the fugitive king and his wine-soaked crony." He gave a mock bow. "Your arrival is so perfectly timely, my lord."

Chapter Five: Trapped

Elak slowly removed his amulet, revealing himself, but as the serpent men stepped forward, he flung it into the face of the first of them, following up with a thrust of his weapon through the eye of the nearest creature. Lycon acted just as swiftly, and in a moment the serpent men found themselves again caught up in a flurry of steel as the Atlanteans cut into them with renewed fury.

"By Bel, I may not have a youth's body, but it's good to be *human* again!" cried Lycon, gleefully running home his blade under the ribs of an opponent.

"Retreat!" shouted Dalan at their shoulder. "We cannot fight them off!"

As one, the trio backed down a passageway that mercifully narrowed: the serpent men could not surround them. Cursing, Scuvular ordered them into the affray. Elak's sword flashed in the grim light, drawing blood, barely one step ahead of his assailants' blades, which hissed through the musty air, narrowly avoiding him, but inching closer.

Dalan barged open a tall doorway in the corridor and the fugitives burst into a long room. The air in here was far colder than it had been outside, the walls gleaming with frost. Dimly, scores of shapes hung from the low ceiling, for a moment seeming like huge, sleeping bats.

"By Ishtar, what are these!" cried Lycon as the three men pushed their way through the shadows. But the things did not move: they were frozen, dead. There was no time to study them for the pursuit was close on their heels, smashing aside the dangling shapes.

But Elak realised what they were—the gutted carcasses of numerous Aquarri, hung up here in cold storage.

"Now you know why they so hate the serpent men," said Dalan beside him, seeing the look of sheer disgust on Elak's face. "They are food for them. This is one larder of many."

Elak had no time to reply, rushing on ahead to another door. He and Lycon kicked in its panels, chopping at its lock. It crashed aside and the trio were out into a corridor almost without a pause. Dalan urged them to follow its downward slope and they did so, the pursuit still hot on their heels.

But ahead of them, lower down in the citadel, they could hear the hiss of yet more serpent men, coming up to meet them. There was a turning to the left of them: cautiously they took it, plunging into darkness. Behind them the serpent men slowed and they heard Scuvular shouting orders amid his curses.

Another door barred the way, this time constructed of thick wood that looked as though it would take more than a good kick to smash it in. Dalan eased his companions aside, told them to shield their faces and then hurled what looked like a ball of scarlet fire at the knotted wood. There was a brief explosion, stars and smoke filled the air, and the door fell inward in a cloud of dust.

Lycon pushed ahead, sensing himself in a tall cavern, but thankfully there was no one in evidence. Quickly the three men began to traverse the stone floor. There was almost no light, just the merest gleam of phosphorescence from the rocks. They had gone some thirty feet into the cavern when they heard a clang of steel behind them. The door through which they had passed was now sealed, for from above it, on this side of the cavern, a huge metal grille had been dropped. Before them they heard another grille fall, doubtless to cut off their forward escape.

Torches abruptly flared above them—by the blazing light of a dozen brands, they now saw themselves to be snared like rabbits in a trap. The chamber was circular, cut from the bedrock, and its two exits were both sealed off by the grilles. The walls of the chamber rose up some twenty feet, the rock as smooth as glass, and above them a narrow balcony overlooked the three fugitives.

And on the balcony the grinning, bloated figure of Scuvular stared down at them. There were a score or more of the serpent men with him, armed with swords and bows. Their arrows pointed menacingly at the three men trapped on the open floor below.

"A laudable attempt at escape," Scuvular mocked. "But for you, Elak, this really is the end of the game. Throw down your weapons!"

Lycon spat and cursed his tormenter loudly and remarkably colourfully.

Dalan slid his weapon into its sheath, face set with a grim resolve. "Do your worst, traitor. These creatures will treat you no better than us when it suits them. Your alliance is founded on vain hopes."

"You think so?" Scuvular mocked. "It is you and your crumbling empire that will go under the waves. Aye, under the waves! Atlantis is the birthright of the strong. She will rise again and be as she was, but not with men ruling her. The serpent men will again rule over her, as they did in the beginning of things. The Old Gods will triumph. Only those who worship them and stand beside their servants, will survive!"

"What have they promised you?" said Elak. "My throne?"

"Yes, and more! They are not yet strong enough to overrun Atlantis, but with my help, they can do so. And when your people have been subjugated, I will yet have a place in their scheme of things. I shall be a demi-god among men! Son of Saaraaza, the Moon God, whose own blood will flow in my veins. And I shall stand beside the monarch, Quarrass-Theen, becoming greatest of his warlords."

"You fool!" snapped Dalan. "You are a *man*! They would never accept you."

"At the ceremony, I will share my blood with theirs. I will be as one with them. And in time, my spawn will be as theirs. A new race begins!" His eyes blazed, his lust for power fuelling his mad devotion, this unspeakable alliance.

"Soon!" he cried, raising his arms to the darkness of the ceiling overhead. "Soon, under the Moon of Saaraaza, your own blood will run, a libation to the Moon God. *When the moon is full, it will begin!*"

Moments later, both Scuvular and his serpent guard had withdrawn from the balcony. A single torch blazed, throwing the cavern into a wavering, garish glow. Lycon quickly went to the steel grilles, but as he expected, both proved unmovable. Elak examined the circular walls, but it was evident that there was no way to shin up them. The trap had been carefully prepared.

"There is no way out," said Dalan, shaking his head.

"Then we'll take as many of them with us as we can down to the Nine Hells!" said Lycon, brandishing his sword.

Elak, for once, had run out of ideas. *When the moon is full,* Scuvular had said. That would be soon indeed, for Quarrass-Theen had said it would be that very night.

Chapter Six: Waters of Death

They could do little else but rest, backs to the stone wall of the chamber. Elak dozed, waking later.

Dalan seemed to be listening to something, intent on sounds that his companions had not heard.

"What is it?" asked Elak.

Dalan rose, face puzzled. "Running water, close at hand."

Lycon grunted. "Aye. There. A grille in the floor. No doubt a river runs below us." His eyes suddenly lit up. *"A river!"* he gasped.

The three of them were at the grille a moment later, but it was secured firmly, locked into the stone. "Even if we were to open this, the water races past, probably deep into the mountains," said Elak.

Dalan motioned for silence, bending low over the grille, apparently listening to the rush of the fuming waters. At length he raised his head, a faint grin on his usually austere features. "They are coming."

Elak and Lycon exchanged puzzled glances, but then Elak realised what the druid meant. "The Aquarri!"

"They know we are here," said Dalan. "If they can reach us, we can free ourselves."

They waited for what seemed an eternity, but at last they could discern movement below the grille. Dalan stood back and the others moved away from him. The druid uttered another spell, hands moving in the air above the grille, which began to glow and then *melt*. In a matter of minutes it had become as soft as cheese, dripping down into the darkness.

Elak leaned over the narrow opening, looking down into the black waters a dozen feet below, where a number of batrachian faces gazed back up at him. He turned to Lycon, grinning. "Are you ready to get wet again?"

"How far?" Lycon asked the druid. "Are you certain we can survive such a plunge?"

"Take a deep breath," said Dalan. "They will guide you to safety."

"Ishtar have pity!" groaned Lycon, but he was first to wriggle through the narrow opening and drop down into the icy waters. Elak and Dalan followed.

As the freezing torrent caught Elak in its grip, tumbling him head over heels, he felt strong hands gripping his arms, guiding him. His head broke the surface in pitch darkness, foam washing over him as he felt himself being hurtled along at frightening speed in the confines of the underground river's passage. On either side of him, more like huge fish than anything else, two of the Aquarri held him up so that he could at least snatch at breaths. Without their help, Elak knew that he would have drowned in moments, that or have been smashed to pulp on the rocky sides of the channel.

After a chaotic plunge through the roaring darkness,

he felt himself spewed out by the torrent into a deep but still lake. The Aquarri urged him upwards and he broke surface with a gasp, dragging more air into his lungs. Not far from his side he heard the garbled curse of Lycon, who had likewise survived the wild journey. Beyond him, Dalan also broke surface. The frog creatures eased all three of them to the sides of the lake, where they gratefully climbed up on to a ledge.

"Where are we now?" Lycon called, gasping for breath.

Dalan spoke softly to the Aquarri, listening to their low, guttural replies. "Beyond the city. Out of sight at least." In the darkness, he took something from the Aquarri: light gleamed briefly on steel. "They retrieved these from your warriors who fell on the surface."

Elak smiled grimly, glad to have a sword in his grasp once more.

"Then let's get back to the surface!" said Lycon. "Bring our forces down here and wipe out this nest of scum!"

"There's no time," said Dalan. "Their ritual will begin soon. If they complete it, no army will stop what the serpent men unleash."

iElak frowned at the druid. "What, exactly, will they unleash?" he asked him.

"I am not sure. But if it is what I think it is, Atlantis as we know it is doomed. We must needs thwart this ritual. It is the only way to stop them."

"So you want to go back to the city?" Lycon groaned. "By Ishtar! This time they'll be waiting for us."

"Granthos and the last of your warriors are not far away," Dalan told Elak. "The Aquarri have brought them to within range of the city. And the Aquarri themselves are gathering. Between us, we can prevent the moon ritual from being fulfilled. After that, we can go back and draw up the army."

"Assuming we survive!" snorted Lycon.

"Seems like we've little choice," said Elak. "What do you want us to do?"

"Go back," said Dalan. Elak nodded and they began the treacherous journey over the rocks and weed along the very edge of the lake. They rounded a shoulder of rock and saw the city ahead of them, its wharfs stretching out into the lake. Far overhead, the vaults of rock that were the ceiling of this huge cavern were cleft in a long gash, revealing a clouded sky, dark grey, its light failing. Evening was drawing on. The moon must have already risen.

"Soon," said Dalan, "the Moon of Saaraaza will be overhead, its light flooding through that opening, spilling on to the place of ritual beneath. It does this each month. So the timing of the ritual is vital to its enactment."

"What is this rite?" said Elak.

"The serpent men will sacrifice to their god. Human blood if they have it."

"So that was to have been our fate?" said Lycon.

"Undoubtedly," nodded Dalan. He said no more, threading his way again through the rocks, under the deep shadows of the lakeside. They reached the very base of one of the stone piers that jutted out into the lake, cloaked in darkness, well hidden from the eyes of the denizens of the city. Out in the lake, they could hear the faint movements in the water that told them the Aquarri were swimming close at hand.

"Well, Lycon," Dalan breathed. "Have you had your fill of water?"

"Bel, yes! I'll freeze if I have to enter it again."

"A short swim," Dalan grinned. "The ritual will take place on yonder island. We must cross to it." He indicated a dark mass some distance across the lake. Torches sputtered at its shore and tall columns rose up at its heart, where an ancient temple had been cut from the stone.

Elak's wolf-like features drew themselves into a scowl that looked even more predatory, his teeth barred, as though he scented his prey and was eager to stalk it to a killing. He nodded at Dalan.

"I'll protect us from the cold as best I can," said the druid, immediately beginning a muttered incantation.

The three men then again took to the waters, easing out silently from the shore, stroking across the darkness towards the island. As they crossed, aware of the Aquarri around them, they saw several flattish barges ferrying serpent men over to the island. They would be there in great force.

Dalan guided his companions around the island and found a sheltered bay, hidden from any prying eyes. The serpent men would have no need to guard this place, so deep in the heart of their own base. All their attention, it now seemed, was focussed on what was happening at the centre of the small island. Rising from the waters like wraiths, Dalan, Elak and Lycon blended with the rocks, slipping in absolute silence upwards into the deeper cover of the broken boulders.

They made their way through them, inching ever closer to the heart of the island. At length they found themselves above the very place of ritual itself. Elak looked down into a circular area that had been completely cleared of rocks to form a flat amphitheatre. Lining it, in a perfect circle, menhirs rose up, arching inward like huge talons. At one end of the circle, a huge statue had been erected. It was cut from a single block of obsidian rock, a bizarre sight, a god unlike any worshipped by men. Its naked body was scaled, its claws webbed, its serpent head elongated, with a long fin running from its crown down its spine and tail.

"Saaraaza," whispered Dalan. "Their Moon God." As he spoke, the clouds far above the split in the cavern ceiling drew aside and the first pale wash of moonlight tinted the sky.

Chapter Seven: Birth of a God

Elak watched as the arena below filled with serpent men: there must have been over a thousand of them, all armed, their lidded eyes fixed on the impassive face of their god. Between the huge carved feet of the massive statue, a long dais stretched out into the arena, like a stone coffin.

"On yonder slab," said Dalan, "they make their sacrifices."

Elak and Lycon watched, grimacing. From the front ranks of the serpent men, a number of figures emerged, resplendent in long robes. One was instantly recognisable as the huge bulk of Quarrass-Theen, Lord of Serpents and ruler of these people. He carried two huge swords and on his brow he wore a golden crown, cast in the shape of a serpent with a wide mouth, twin fangs poised as if to strike. On either side of him were two beings that Elak assumed to be his high priests, their thick arms banded with gold, their own brows crowned with serpent diadems.

And the final figure to emerge from the host was Scuvular. He was bareheaded, but he wore splendid robes, fit for a king. He smiled up at the god-statue, but there was a look of nervousness about him, surrounded as he was by so many of the scaly warriors.

All became motionless, silent, as the priests took up their places beside the huge slab of stone, the place of power—sorcery that pulsed and throbbed in the night air like a vital force, ready to be directed. Quarrass-Theen held aloft his twin swords, his face raised up to the opening high overhead. By the glow there it was apparent that the moon was moving across the external heavens to the point at which it would be visible to the company in the arena, directly overhead. Its light would shine straight down upon the sacrificial slab.

"We venerate thee, Saaraaza!" came the deep voice of the Lord of Serpents. "Your children are gathered at thy feet! Bathe us in your glory and make us strong. We offer up to you our power. We exalt you among gods and give to you this Atlantis! We give back to you what is yours,

stolen from you by the spawn of false gods on the earth!"

As he spoke, the rim of the moon, brilliant and full, edged across the high opening like a curve of pure gold, an immense, god-like eye.

"To symbolise our dominion over Man, we have brought this servant before you," Quarrass-Theen intoned, indicating the uneasy form of Scuvular. "We will make him more than a leader of Men, more than their king! Tonight, under your glow, illustrious Saaraaza, *we will make him a god!*"

It was all that Lycon could do to keep silent at this blasphemy. Elak gripped his arm tightly, shaking his head.

Scuvular's face could be seen clearly in the waxing moonlight, suffused now with greedy pleasure, unholy joy at the gift bestowed upon him.

"Scuvular will be a god among Men!" repeated Quarrass-Theen. "They will bow to him and he will serve us as we rule over Atlantis once more." The huge serpent man turned again to Scuvular. The twin blades fell gently on to his shoulders. From among the gathered serpent warriors, a cry of jubilation went up.

"I venerate thee, Saaraaza!" Scuvular cried, head thrown back, neck exposed so that the full glow of the moon fell upon it.

"By Ishtar!" gasped Elak, realising what was about to happen. "He's to become a god, yes, but they're going to spill his blood on the altar! Deification through the ritual of death! His blood is the fuel that will ignite these abominable powers!"

"We will give blood to the Moon God!" cried Quarrass-Theen. "Blood that his power may be exercised this night."

In a blur of movement, the two serpent priests gripped Scuvular's arms and dragged him to the slab of sacrifice, abruptly yanking him backwards so that he fell on to his back, the nape of his neck hitting the edge of the slab. His head lolled back, eyes widening in sudden realisation and sheer horror. Held in a grip of iron, he could not move.

"Scuvular, by this act, you become a god among Men, a servant of Saaraaza. Your blood will give him the power to reach out to us."

The moon had shifted across the opening high above, almost filling it. Its light fell upon the struggling form of Scuvular, his neck exposed to the blade that lifted over it.

"Power!" repeated Quarrass-Theen. "Saaraaza, you are closer to this world at this moment than you have been for a thousand years! Accept your sacrifice. Drink the blood and fuel yourself with the power! Come closer yet through this act."

Beside Elak, Dalan gasped, understanding striking him like a physical blow. "*Closer!* Gods, they mean to bring the moon *closer.*"

"What does it mean?" said Elak.

"The tides!" said the druid in horror. "The moon governs the tides. If it draws closer to us, the tides of the Earth will *rise.*"

Elak gasped. The threat that ever hung over Atlantis——that she would sink beneath the waves——would be realised.

"Epharra, your city port," said Dalan, "The ports of Kornak, San-Mu and even great Poseidonia itself, all will be covered by the ocean. Most of the population dwells on or close to the coasts. A small sea rise would wipe them out and what would be left——"

"Would be easy prey for these reptiles," nodded Elak.

There was no time to think. Elak could see the great sword of Quarrass-Theen rising to the tip of an arc, about to plunge down and spill the vital blood of Scuvular. The Lord of the Serpents paused for a brief moment, waiting for the Moon God to move into the precise location in the heavens. Then the blade began its descent.

Elak leapt to his feet, bending his back like a huge bow: he flung his own sword end over end. Moonlight shone upon it as it hissed through the air. It took seconds only for it to reach its target—the forearm of Quarrass-Theen. Whether through luck or the will of Ishtar, the point of Elak's blade found its mark, sinking in and through the thick arm of the serpent ruler. His ritual blade fell from a limp claw, its edge crashing into the stone of the slab, inches from Scuvular's exposed neck. Sparks flew and in the consternation the priests eased their grip on Scuvular, who immediately tore free of them and swung off the sacrificial slab.

Quarrass-Theen screamed like a demon, blood dripping from his wound, his arm useless. He gaped up at the moon, but already it was sliding across the opening in the cavern roof. In a few moments it would have passed. Scuvular snatched a sword from one of the bemused priests and used it to deadly effect, ramming it up to the hilt in the creature's gut. He turned to face the gathered serpent men, all of whom were now snarling like maddened hounds at the sacrilege.

"Come!" said Dalan. "If the traitor dies now, it will not serve their cause. They have lost their opportunity. We must get away."

Elak shook his head. "No, we must finish this. In another month they can do it all again! Scuvular must die, as must the Lord of Serpents." Without another word, he leapt across the rocks and began the descent down into the arena.

Lycon's simian features screwed up into what passed for a grin. "By the Nine Hells, it's as good a time as any to die!" he growled and followed his master into the confusion below.

Elak was at the rear of the slab before anyone had noticed him, his sword cutting down the second of the priests before the serpent was even aware that he was under attack. Scuvular saw what had happened, realising how he had been rescued. But there was no time to discuss it. He backed towards Elak, fending off a half-dozen blades.

Dalan watched from above as the trio of men formed a circle and defended themselves against a furious onslaught. He studied the unequal battle for no more than a few moments, then turned and disappeared into the night, unseen by the serpent men.

Beneath him they closed in for the certain kill.

Chapter Eight: Eye of the God

The space behind the sacrificial slab and the great statue of Saaraaza was cramped, but it worked to the advantage of the three men as their swords rose and fell incessantly. Serpent men fell before that dazzling web of steel, Elak roaring his defiance in the face of death. But he knew that the numbers facing him would eventually overwhelm him and the men beside him.

Quarrass-Theen, still clutching his ruined, dripping arm, screamed orders from behind the slab, keeping himself out of the way of the swords of his enemies. But as the serpents pressed harder, sure of their victory, a new outcry rose from the edge of the arena, near its stone gates.

The serpents were under attack from behind! Elak craned his neck and could just discern a mass of hundreds of the Aquarri which had boiled in from outside. Although each of them was half the size of the huge serpent men, they tore into them like a pack of wild hounds, small swords and tridents jabbing, ripping. For vital moments the attention of the serpent men was snared and Elak used the time to leap up on to the slab, cut down two of them and jump down beside Quarrass-Theen.

But the huge Lord of the Serpents was still a dangerous foe, despite having but one arm to defend himself with. He used his second sword to block all Elak's attempts to bring him down, backing off towards the press of his own warriors. Steel rang and the air was rich with curses as the two fought with a terrible tenacity, their eyes locked, gleaming with an ancient hatred that had festered over untold centuries during the endless war between their kinds. It was enough to buy Quarrass-Theen time, for several of his closest warriors stepped in between him and Elak, protecting their Lord.

From above the arena, scores more of the Aquarri appeared, carrying with them light bows, and they unleashed wave after wave of arrows down into the packed, confused mass of the serpent men. Many of the latter fell, or turned to flee the arrows only to be met with the steel of the Aquarri coming in from the gates. Untold numbers of the sea creatures had now amassed and, although many of them were cut down and trampled by the serpent men, they refused to withdraw.

Scuvular found himself temporarily free of opponents, for the serpent men who had been attacking him were more concerned with defending their ruler. They had turned upon Elak, who, from the corner of his eye, watched in consternation as not only Quarrass-Theen but also the traitor prepared to make a bolt for it.

But Lycon appeared out of the shadows before Scuvular. "Not leaving so soon, Scuvular? You still think to steal a crown? Not while I draw breath, you vermin!"

Scuvular cursed, defending himself anew against an even more ferocious attack as Lycon pressed him hard.

Elak drove back his opponents, trying to see where Quarrass-Theen had gone. There was nowhere for the huge serpent man to run: his own forces were so packed together, hemmed in by the hordes of Aquarri to form a solid wall. But he was cutting a swath through the Aquarri towards the gateway. Overhead the indifferent moon had gone, leaving only a dim glow in the opening to the skies. A few stars looked down upon the bloody events.

Elak drove hard into the reptile men, but the royal guards were possessed of extraordinary strength. With a sudden twist of his blade, their leader struck Elak's sword aside and drove him to his knees, sensing a victory.

"Your ritual is over!" came a voice beyond the serpent man, halting him. He swung round, eyes blazing.

Lycon, face splattered with blood and sweat, held up a grisly trophy. "Here is your erstwhile Moon God." And he flung the severed head of Scuvular into the face of the serpent guards.

As the huge beings ducked instinctively aside, Elak snatched up his fallen sword and drove its point up under the jaw of the first of them, grinding on bone and brain. A deafening, shrill hiss escaped from the being and he sagged to his knees, the light in his eyes dimming.

BY ADRIAN COLE

Elak drew out the sword and made to strike again, but he knew that the Lord of Serpents had escaped him, cutting his way to a barge down on the edge of the island. The last of his company protected him, fighting their way out, though many of them yet fell to the determined Aquarri.

Dalan watched the flight of the Lord of Serpents before entering the arena and going to where Elak and Lycon stood, their chests heaving, sword arms limp at their sides.

"Any longer," gasped Lycon, "and I'd have dropped from sheer exhaustion."

"The Aquarri fought like demons," said Elak. "But so many of them died." He pointed at the piles of slain, many of whom were the diminutive frog figures. As suddenly as it had begun, the battle was over.

Dalan stood over the corpse of Scuvular. "For the Aquarri it was a worthy sacrifice. A dreadful ritual has been thwarted. This monster was the greatest threat the serpent men have brought upon mankind for many years. That and the fierce will of Quarrass-Theen. Only his desire for conquest drove them on. It will be long before they feel strong enough to rise up again."

"In which case," said Lycon, "it really must be time to get back to the surface. If I don't get a drink soon, I'll evaporate."

Elak's face clouded. "There's more bloody work yet. The Lord of Serpents fled. We must pursue him and put an end to him."

One of the Aquarri came to Dalan and exchanged guttural words with him.

"What is it?" said Elak, sensing the druid's unease.

"Granthos. Your other warriors. The serpents have them in the citadel. They were on the way to find you, but were outnumbered."

Elak wiped his blade, nodding. "Very well. Let us settle this once and for all."

Chapter Nine: Citadel of Evil

It was long gone midnight and the darkness of the cavern was absolute. If there were torches lit down below in the serpent citadel, they were not visible from up here on the heights. Lycon swore, almost slipping to his doom on the dangerous outcrop. But Elak gripped his arm and swung him to safety.

"Here is a way in," said Dalan, indicating an even blacker cleft in the rocks.

They were far above the city, close to where the rushing torrents that plunged downward into its drains emerged from the upper layers of rock, though still far below the surface of the outer world. It had been Elak's idea to come here.

"We must enter the city secretly," he had said. "Can we not do so the same way we left it, through the underground river?"

After considerable thought, Dalan had shaken his head. "There are many grilles, but they are all many feet above the water level, except possibly in the spring thaws. And the waters race past them."

"Why not use the serpents' own tricks against them?" Elak had grinned, a sudden idea coming to him. "They sought to raise the tides. Can we not *divert* the river? Send it along some other course and empty its bed under the citadel?"

Dalan had been dubious at first but, after a discussion with the Aquarri, had agreed that it might be possible. Thus a large host of the small creatures had gone up into the heights and had ultimately found a place where the diversion could be achieved. Now, entering the cleft in the rocks, Dalan led his companions along a narrow crevice into the interior.

They heard the rush of waters at once and saw the glow of torches where the Aquarri awaited them. They were on a ledge, near which the waters tumbled in a white spray down to a narrow pool that emptied into a tunnel mouth that had the symmetrical curve of an artificial opening.

"See," said Dalan. "When the city was built, its architects diverted these waters down through yonder tunnel. It feeds the drains of the city."

"Can we divert the river?" said Elak.

Dalan nodded thoughtfully. At once he set the Aquarri to work, moving boulders, levering slabs of stone from the walls, Elak and Lycon helping them, using their swords as tools. It was arduous and time-consuming, but in an hour they had shifted enough stone to make an impact. Dalan waved everyone back and called upon his dark arts to complete the work. A sudden blast of fire and light removed a mass of overhanging rock and, as it tumbled into the river, the waters drove countless tons of material forward. They heaped up before the tunnel opening, and the river split in two, tumbling away into the deep wells of darkness on either side of the drain system.

Lycon grimaced. "Done! Is it safe to go into that tunnel? Looks like a death trap!"

"The Aquarri will lead us," said Dalan.

Moments later the company climbed down into the silt and, mindful of the treacherous footing, went under the stone overhang. Dalan held up a torch and by its sputtering glow they could see that the way down was steep, slick with mud, but not impassable. Slowly they began the perilous descent. Somewhere close by, on either side, they could hear the muffled roar of the diverted waters, plunging downward.

It took another hour to get far enough down the precipitous tunnel to reach the outer citadel itself. The floor was less steep, very little silt here due to the previous speed of the flow. But they kept looking back, knowing that, should the river find a way of restoring its path, they would be swept to their doom. Even the Aquarri would not be able to withstand the first mighty thrust of the returning waters.

As they dropped lower, the tunnel got larger, its ceiling higher above them. It presented a new problem, for as Dalan had surmised, the grilles that now appeared in the floor of the chambers of the city were out of reach. Just as they had begun to resign themselves to defeat, one of the Aquarri led them to a grille set in the side wall of the tunnel. It was the act of a moment to rip the rusting mesh away. The vent that was exposed turned out to be a drain up into what must be a washroom or bathhouse.

Elak wriggled up the slippery tunnel and came to another grille. The room beyond was dark and silent. He pushed the grille up and entered the room, which contained several large baths. There was a central floor grille and, removing this, he peered down into the torch glow to see his companions below. He waved them up and, although Lycon found the drain barely large enough to accommodate his bulk, he finally squeezed through it and into the bathhouse.

"Where are we?" Elak asked Dalan. "How close to the heart of the citadel?"

Dalan was studying the walls of the room. "The gods may have smiled upon us. This is no simple bathhouse. We are in the royal apartments! Our friends have not let us down," he added, indicating the dozen or so Aquarri who had accompanied them this far.

"Then Quarrass-Theen could be close at hand?"

"Let us tread softly." Dalan led them to the door, easing it open. The corridor beyond was not lit, so the druid's own torch picked out the bare details. The company moved like spectres, along several corridors until they came to a wider one. Two huge serpent guards leaned on its walls, but they were slumped, dozing, not expecting intruders in this secluded part of their citadel.

They were dead before they could come fully awake.

Elak stood outside the tall door, its intricate work suggesting that this was the way to a room of some impor-

tance. He glanced at Dalan. The druid nodded.

Elak thrust at the door and it opened with a protesting groan. Beyond were the anticipated royal apartments, their centrepiece a huge oval bed. Slumped across it was the huge shape of Quarrass-Theen. He was alone.

"Kill him," Lycon whispered beside Elak. "One quick thrust——"

Elak grimaced, not eager to strike in cold blood, in spite of the need to end the serpent men threat. But he moved silently towards the huge bed.

The Lord of the Serpents sat upright, reaching out for the long sword beside the huge divan. He rolled over and on to his feet in one swift move, like a wild beast at bay.

Elak grinned, his own blade extended. "It ends here, Quarrass-Theen."

The serpent man's damaged arm hung uselessly at his side, heavily bandaged, but he was still a considerable threat, his huge height and weight advantage over Elak more than compensating for the loss of the use of one arm. With a snarl of fury, he leapt forward, the sword flashing in the torchlight.

Chapter Ten: Wrath of the Gods

Lycon was barely able to hold back, but Dalan stayed him, watching the two warriors as they came together in a clash of steel that rang back from the chamber walls. It was to be a test of Elak's agility and speed against the sheer brute strength and fury of the Lord of Serpents and rarely had two warriors been so well matched.

The huge sword of the serpent man chopped down in a blur and narrowly missed cleaving Elak open from shoulder to waist as he slipped aside, his own rapier darting forward like a snake's tongue to tear through the scales of his opponent's side, though inflicting no more than superficial damage. Backwards and forwards the fight raged, both protagonists seeming to get the upper hand, only to surrender it again.

Quarrass-Theen had moved back deeper into the chamber. Behind the divan was a long curtain and he cut it down with a single sweep of his blade to reveal an open doorway beyond. Elak could see that this led out on to a balcony and over a narrow bridge to yet another tall chamber. The Lord of Serpents meant to withdraw across the bridge to this. The bridge spanned a narrow corridor that debouched into darkness on either side some twenty feet below.

Elak allowed the serpent man to go out on to the balcony and step on to the bridge, pressing his advantage.

Beyond the span, a door swung open with a crash and three serpent guards came out on to the bridge's far side, swords poised. They called to their ruler, who snarled a command.

"Finish him!" shouted Lycon to Elak, himself rushing forward, but on the span there was room for one only to pass. "If he crosses, we'll lose him."

Elak was about to press forward, when a roaring sound to his left made him swing round. Somewhere in the darkness there was a noise like a storm, as if outside the walls of the chamber thunder was raging. But down here in the bowels of the earth that was not possible, Elak knew.

Quarrass-Theen, now at the center of the span, also turned to see what caused the roar. As he did so, huge bricks tumbled forward out of the darkness in an explosion of spray and foam.

"The river!" cried Dalan. "Elak, get back!"

Elak needed no second bidding, leaping back to the balcony and into the bedchamber. Outside he saw the abrupt surge of water, a boiling, tumbling wave, come smashing through the far wall of the passageway. As it tore past, the pent up power of the diverted underground river unleashed itself and swept down the passage like the fist of a god. Quarrass-Theen, trapped on the span, was smashed from it, stricken like a fly and flung forward.

Elak saw the huge serpent man crushed up to the far wall of the passage, tossed upwards in the seething foam once, twice, then again, before being sucked down into the river and onwards as it ripped out its new course through the citadel, punching aside everything in its path.

Beyond the span, which had been torn from its foundations and hurled after the broken Lord of Serpents, the three guards had also been plunged into the torrent.

Elak turned at last to his companions, satisfied that his enemies had been swept away to oblivion. "An unexpected ally—or did you plan that, Dalan?"

The druid shook his head. "Not I. But the gods of Atlantis still watch over her, it would seem."

"Come, then," said Elak. "Let us find Granthos and the others."

They left the chamber, racing down several corridors. Further in the citadel's heart, the abrupt flood had wrought havoc and the serpent men who had been stationed here had either been swept away or knocked senseless. The few that had survived were no match for the Aquarri who dealt with them as ruthlessly as the river had done.

Dalan was brought to an area below the royal chambers, a series of cells in which Granthos and his companions had been imprisoned. Once the keys to the doors were found and the cells opened, it was the work of a moment for Elak to reunite himself with his men.

"We heard what sounded like a thunderstorm, *within* the citadel!" said Granthos as Elak hugged him.

"The gods have flushed out this place," nodded Elak.

*　　*　　*　　*　　*

Later, on the shores of the lake, the company said their farewells to the Aquarri. The corpses of Quarrass-Theen and his principal warriors had all been found, tangled at the lowest tier of the citadel, bodies broken and lifeless.

One of the Aquarri came to Lycon and handed to him a clay jar.

"What's this?"

"A reward for your efforts on their behalf," said Dalan. "I warrant you'll not find another vintage of wine like it in all Atlantis."

Lycon prized up the cork and sniffed. He shook his head, simian features drawn into a terrifying frown. "Judging by the fumes, I'd say you are right."

"And I'd say," Elak told Dalan quietly, "that by the time we reach the surface, he'll have forgotten the fumes and quaffed the lot."

"Then we'll be carrying him home. That is potent stuff," Dalan grunted.

"And I'll wager you a bag of gold that he'll be calling for another."

IN AN OCTOPUS'S GARDEN

by Kevin L. O'Brien

illustrated by Alex McVey

Editor's Note: On March 1, 2000, Joshua and Victoria Matisse (not their real names) set sail from San Francisco on a six month cruise through the central and south Pacific. On board they had a satellite telephone, and they called their parents at least once a week. They reached the State of Pohnpei, the largest island in the Federated States of Micronesia, on April 3rd; on April 5th they left for a nearby atoll they had rented. They were last heard from on May 6th. By May 21st their parents contacted their Congressman, who in turn convinced the State Department to launch an investigation. On June 9th a team lead by an attaché arrived at Pohnpei and remained for a week, conducting the investigation with the cooperation of the Pohnpei governor's office, before returning to the US. Though they verified that the Matisses had arrived at Pohnpei, they found no trace of them at the atoll, with the major exception of a handwritten manuscript allegedly written by Joshua Matisse hidden in a hollowed-out coconut buried beneath a small stone cairn.

The State Department eventually issued a report which stated that experts were unable to verify the authenticity of the manuscript. Accordingly, it concluded that there was no evidence that the Matisses had ever visited the atoll. It further speculated that they may have deliberately misled their parents for the purposes of staging a disappearance, but in any event they were simply declared missing. The case was closed, pending an investigation by the Justice Department into Victoria Matisse's trading practices at the brokerage firm she worked for.

What follows is the text of the manuscript. No changes have been made, except that underlines have been converted to italics. It has been released for publication by the parents of the couple in the hope that someone may have information regarding the fate or whereabouts of the Matisses. If anyone reading this has such information, please contact the publishers of this magazine.

I don't know if anyone will find this testament. I've already split and cleaned out the coconut, dug the hole, and gathered the stones; all I need to do the writing. The problem is they may find it, but if I hide it too well no one else will. So I have to take the chance.

I'm getting ahead of myself. Let me start at the beginning. Vicki and I had been married for five years, but we could never conceive any children. Not that we weren't trying; we made love three times a week and twice on weekends. But nothing seemed to work. We went to our doctor to ask about alternatives. He wanted to give us a physical before he discussed that, but afterwards he pronounced us in perfect health. He thought it might be stress. We were both rather busy with our respective professions, so it made sense to us. He suggested we take some time off; if that didn't work, then he would be willing to try some fertility drugs.

We had always wanted to take a sailing tour of the South Pacific, but to do it right we would have to take several months off. We didn't have enough vacation time accumulated, but we talked it over and decided to each take a leave of absence, since we had enough savings to cover it. So we arranged with our respective employers to take six months off. After that it was a simple matter to rent a boat and set up our itinerary. One thing we really wanted to do was find some place where we could rent an island or something. While we didn't plan to waste any nights on the boat, we wanted to spend some time in a romantic location where we didn't have to wear anything except suntan lotion and we didn't have to do anything except have sex. Unfortunately, that proved more difficult. Fortunately our travel agent knew of a realtor on an island called Ponape in the East Caroline Islands that could rent us a small atoll. So we made a reservation and paid a retainer.

The boat itself was a single-masted schooner with an inboard motor, an onboard computer and GPS tracking system, and a radio with a satellite phone. It had a single spacious cabin, a galley, and a lavatory, plus an expansive afterdeck. Both Vicki and I were experienced yachtsmen in college; in fact, that was how we first met, as rivals in a regatta. We tied for first place. So while it had been some time since we last did any sailing, it was the kind of boat we were used to, and we doubted that we would have any problems.

We left San Francisco at the beginning of March and headed towards Hawaii. We took our time crossing the Pacific; we weren't in any hurry. We intended to cut ourselves off from home entirely, but the one concession we made was to our parents. They were worried that we might run into trouble being on our own for so long, so we promised to call them not less than once a week. We spent a week touring the Hawaiian Islands, then swung south and west towards the Marshalls. We spent another week working our way up the chain before heading west and south towards Ponape. We finally arrived after the beginning of April in the mid afternoon. The island was a round, low volcano that looked more like a mound of dirt. It was surrounded by a barrier reef, but there were several passages through it. We used the Mwand pass, then made our way west around the north end of the island to the smaller Sokehs Island. We sailed down the west side into the Sokehs Harbor and finally moored at a marina run by the South Park Hotel.

We went ashore into Kolonia, which was the capital town, and went straight to the realtor. We paid the remainder of the rental and she gave us a map and navigational information to the atoll. She was pleasant enough, but there was something faintly repellent about her. It might have been her sallow skin or her bulging eyes, but I now remember she had a barely detectable fishy smell. Afterwards, we ate at the hotel restaurant and celebrated our arrival in one of their rooms.

The next morning we toured the town, seeing the old Spanish fortifications and the Japanese gun emplacements from World War II. Then we visited the Lidudubniap waterfall and the Nan Madol ruins. These were very interesting. According to the tour guide, millennia ago a mysterious race of people built artificial islands offshore in the lagoon and then placed buildings on them. From a distance they looked like they were built of wood logs, but up close we were astonished to see that the "logs" were made of stone! Basalt in fact, according to the guide. Most of the buildings were modest in size, but several were quite large, and one was huge. No one knew who the people were or how they could have cut and shaped the "logs" or assembled them, but Ponape legend told that a race of demons called the *saudeleurs* built the ruins. They were described as being some kind of cross between humans and octopi, and they supposedly worshipped some kind of water god called Katoluha. It all sounded pretty farfetched to me, but then I suppose any mythology would.

When we returned to the hotel, we discussed the possibility of staying an extra day to do some snorkeling, but we quickly decided against it. We were eager to get to the atoll and we could always do our snorkeling there. When we weren't busy with other activities. So we checked out of the hotel, spent the evening buying supplies, and slept out on the boat.

Early next morning we set sail. We left through the Pehleng passage and turned south before going east around the island. Once we were out into the ocean proper, for the first time during the trip so far we used the engine continuously instead of just for maneuvers. It was a waste of fuel, we knew, but we wanted to get there as soon as possible. We sailed due east for a day and half before we sighted a small collection of coral islands. The atoll was only a mile in diameter, and the largest island covered barely a third of the circumference, but it was lush with vegetation and there was a Polynesian bungalow as promised. The lagoon was crystal clear, all the way down to the bottom, and the water turquoise in contrast to the deep, dark blue of the surrounding ocean.

We made a quick tour of the islands. With the exception of two others, all were simply exposed mounds of coral of various sizes, and those two were barely a quarter of the size of the main island and had only a few coconut trees. What surprised us, however, was that on each of these two islands was a structure almost identical to the ones we saw at Nan Madol. We were tempted to stop and investigate, but again we were eager to get settled in and begin what we came to do, and besides we would have four weeks to do whatever exploring we wished. So we headed straight across the lagoon towards the main island. I'm convinced now that had we not done so, we would never have seen the tower.

Fortunately, Vicki was standing on the prow as I steered. We had by this time stripped down to bathing suits, and Vicki had also removed her top. I watched her standing up there, as she stared out ahead of us. She was gorgeous, and this trip had only improved her. She was tall and slim, trim and muscular from her daily workouts, and she had a rich, golden tan unmarred by bathing suit shadow. Her legs were long and shapely, and her magnificent rear was accentuated by the thong bottom she wore. As she shifted position I occasionally caught sight of a swell of breast. They were not large, but they were firm, and she was most proud of them. She had cut her red-bronze hair short to be more comfortable in the tropical climate, but it swayed and bounced with each slight movement. Though she had her back to me, I could easily picture her strong, beautiful features in her round face.

Suddenly she turned and waved at me. For a moment I didn't notice, because while, like me, she wore sunglasses, I was imagining her gold-brown eyes. Then I heard her shouting.

"Joshua. Joshua! Hard to port! To *port!*"

Snapping out of my daydream, I spun the wheel frantically as Vicki gestured vigorously to the left and braced

herself. The ship lurched toward that side, and I saw her stare off to starboard, her eyes following something as it past. I looked as well, and saw a thin pinnacle about three feet high sticking up out of the water. I looked at Vicki in astonishment, but she just smiled and shrugged before turning back towards the front.

We reached the main island with no further incident and weighed anchor just offshore, then furled the sail. When we had stowed all the gear we were no longer going to need for awhile, we looked at each other. There was no need to say a word; we both knew what was on each other's mind. We quickly shed the last of our clothing and packed it away. We had no intention of wearing any clothes as long as we stayed here. We then spread a blanket on the forward deck, spread suntan lotion over every inch of our bodies until we were glistening and slippery, and got immediately to work.

It was the best sex we had had since we were first married. We seemed to have boundless energy and in this private place we abandoned all inhibitions. When we were dating, we preferred to make love on one of our boats; that way we could vent our passion fully. After we were married, however, we sold the boats to purchase a condo. Unfortunately, our neighbors were light sleepers and often complained about the noise we made. So we were forced to moderate our actions. Now, for the first time in years, our bodies writhed in frenzied rapture and we cried out our ecstasy loudly, in tones that rang across the lagoon. Our ardor did not weaken and our manic fervor lasted well into the night, when finally we exploded with an intensity that convulsed us, and we collapsed exhausted into each other's embrace.

Vicki soon fell asleep in my arms, her head on my chest just under my chin, but I lay awake for a little while afterward, gazing up at the night sky. I had lived in a city all my life, so I never really looked at the stars. Here they were so clear they blazed forth like brilliant diamonds, and there were hundreds of them. The Milky Way stretched across the heavens like a diffuse, dusty path, and meteorites crisscrossed it frequently. Vicki's warm weight felt good on top of me, and I held her close. I felt a comfortable warm afterglow of drowsy pleasure that settled within me, weighing me down towards sleep. I remember thinking, *This is what Heaven must be like*. Then I closed my eyes and let myself drift off to sleep, as the boat rocked gently beneath us.

We spent the next two weeks engaging in mad, passionate, animal sex. We would make love for two or three days straight, stopping only to eat, and sleeping only when we exhausted ourselves. Then we would spend a day or two recuperating. At those times we would dive the lagoon. It was beautiful, like a fantastic fairy garden. Vicki and I had dived coral reefs before, but none was as spectacular as this. To begin with, the water was so clear it was as if it wasn't even there. Sunlight flooded undiminished even to the very bottom, and the wavelets cast beaded patterns of bright reflection alternating with dark shadows rippling across everything. The coral was brightly colored, like beds of gems and precious stones, like hedges covered with beautiful multicolored flowers in a terrestrial ornamental garden. Fish flitted about the corals like birds, only they were by far more exquisite than any avian could be. The only thing missing was gay song, but we found that a minor inconvenience.

There were, however, two oddities. The first was the total, though welcome, lack of any major predators: no sharks, no barracudas, no moray eels. The other was the octopi. The lagoon was filled with them. They ranged in size from no bigger than our hands to near the size of the giant octopus in the northern Pacific. And they were all extremely beautiful. Like any cephalopod they could change colors and patterns instantly, one moment gaudily decorated like rainbow harlequins, the next so perfectly camouflaged we couldn't see them even up close. They were also shy, but only at first. Once they got used to us they seemed to look forward to our visits, and they were very playful and quite smart. We enjoyed our time among them almost as much as our marathon sex episodes.

Being as the ship's cabin was fairly cramped, we spent most of our nights on deck. We fixed up a bed of sorts using cushions, pillows, and blankets. It wasn't the best we could have done, but it was sufficiently comfortable. Yet sometimes, for a change a pace, or when it rained (as it did on rare occasions), we slept inside the bungalow. We didn't do it often, though, because it was even more uncomfortable than our makeshift deck bed. Still, it gave us an excuse to explore the island. There wasn't much to it, however, and the jungle was thick and overrun with crabs, so we avoided it for the most part. One morning, however, Vicki awoke me urgently. She often rose before I did and spent some time jogging around the island before making breakfast.

"Josh. Josh! Wake up, I've found something!"

I came out of my sleep with a fuzzy head, and tried to embrace her.

"No, not that," she laughed, pushing me away, "not now. Come on, get up; it's important." And with that she dashed out to wait for me. When I finally woke up completely I followed her out and found her waiting for me on the beach. I asked her what was up.

In reply she jogged off to the left, waving for me to follow. I did, and we went about half way around the island before she stopped and started searching the jungle. By the time I caught up, she found what she was looking for and pointed it out: a trail barely a foot wide. Before I could stop her she started down it, pushing through the bushes. I went in after her, trying to catch her, but she managed to stay just out of reach. Then she seemed to disappear right in front of my eyes. I panicked and rushed forward, crashing through a wall of heavy brush, and I found myself in a clearing. Ahead of me Vicki was dancing around a crowd of crabs as she made for a structure that sat at the center. It looked exactly like the buildings we saw at the Nan Madol ruins, right down to the basalt logs it was constructed from. It was designed as a low rectangular box with a high, peaked roof. The only opening I could see was just above where the roof sat on the box. Even as I watched, Vicki reached the building and began climbing the logs towards the entrance. I yelled at her to stop, to wait for me, but she either didn't hear or was ignoring me.

I ran after her, dodging crabs, and I reached the structure just as she disappeared inside. I started climbing then, but was relieved to see Vicki stick her head out the opening and look for me. When I reached her she helped me in, then left me to catch my breath. I watched her as she walked around the interior. The openings between the logs let in enough sunlight to see clearly, and my eyes soon adjusted to the lower light level. The box beneath us had been filled with some kind of gravel, most likely coral, right up to the roof level. In the center several logs had been laid side by side to form a platform, and six logs had been set upright into the rubble around it in a rough circle. Stone slabs had been leaned against the roof walls along both sides. Otherwise the space was empty.

While Vicki examined the posts, I went over to look at the slabs. They were rough hewn from basalt, about three feet long by a foot and a half wide, but their faces were smoothed and highly polished. As I squatted down I saw that letters were chiseled into the faces, and I was astonished when I realized that I recognized them! My profession is linguistics, and I specialize in Polynesian and its various dialects. That was one reason why I wanted to tour the South Pacific (though Vicki would have killed me if I had turned this into a working vacation). The only known writing system for any member of the Polynesian language group was Rongorongo, the script invented by the Rapa Nui of Easter Island sometime in the late eighteenth century. Yet there persisted rumors of crystal tablets, found inside lava bombs thrown out of a volcano in Hawaii during an eruption sometime in the seventeenth century, that were inscribed with a script that was suppose to be a written form of the ancient root language of the Polynesian group. I had seen photographs reputed to be of the "Kuhalai tablets" as they were known, as well the transcripts of the supposed translation, but like virtually all my colleagues I assumed it was just a hoax. Now here I was confronted with proof it was not. It made me wish I had paid more attention to those transcripts.

I called to Vicki to come over and see them. When she didn't respond, I turned to look for her. I found her standing on the platform in the center of the posts. A shaft of light illuminated her, and she glistened with sweat. It was rather warm and humid inside the structure, which I thought was unusual since we had been surprised by how mild the climate around the atoll was. I was about to call her again when I saw she was rubbing herself provocatively. That startled me, but as I watched her it turned me on. She turned around then and stared at me lasciviously, licking her lips. I strolled over to her, strutting, showing myself off. She crooked a finger at me with one hand and touched herself with the other. When I stepped past the posts into their center, a wave of lustfulness washed over me. We practically threw ourselves into each other's arms and we made love on the platform.

From then on we slept together inside the structure, day or night, rain or shine; we even went so far as to move our deck bed there. Our sex seemed more intense, yet we also seemed to have more stamina. I swear, sometimes we seemed to be able to make love for twenty-fours straight.

The only drawback was that our dreams began at that time as well.

They were pleasant enough at first: we swam through the lagoon, breathing the water like we were fish. We made friends with the octopi, and they told us stories. They told us how ages ago great beings came down out of the heavens and strode over the surface of the earth. They built gigantic cities and taught the octopi how to sing and dance; in gratitude they served and worshiped

BY KEVIN L. O'BRIEN

the beings. Then the stars changed, and the beings fell into a death-like sleep. The octopi built tombs for them, and placed them inside; they told us that one of those tombs was located here in this lagoon, in its center where it was deepest, and that they watch over it, until the time when the stars would be right again, and the beings would awaken to once more stride over the earth.

At first we played games with them, sang with them, joined them in their dances, and always listened to their awesome stories, but as the dreams continued we began to, I guess I have to say it, *copulate* with them. They would entwine their bodies with ours and caress us, and we would become enflamed with passion and surrender ourselves to them.

After a short while they began taking us deeper into the lagoon. When we dived it while awake we pretty much restricted ourselves to a shallow shelf within a hundred yards of shore, so we never discovered that just beyond it the bottom began to slope down to a deeper shelf surrounding an abyss at the center. There we found buildings that clustered right up to the edge of the pit. They were constructed of bricks made from a greenish stone with silvery veins, but their design was bizarre. It defied every principle of Euclidean geometry, and the shape of the buildings seemed to twist and distort as our view of them changed. But that may have simply been because the light was weaker here and it was harder to see them distinctly.

The city had been built by the saudeleurs, we were told. When the beings had been active they had taken certain of the octopi and had changed them to better serve their masters. These became the saudeleurs. Though extremely long-lived, they were unfortunately not immortal like the beings, nor could they reproduce on their own, so when their masters fell into their death-sleep, no new saudeleurs were made, and their numbers began to dwindle over time. Now there were only a handful left. The octopi took us to meet them, out of reverence and respect, because the octopi worshiped them as gods, even as they worshiped the beings. We met them in an open space that I supposed was a meeting place. We stood in the center, holding hands, waiting for them; then they emerged from the gloom one at a time. Their appearance that first time startled us awake, but we could still remember it vividly.

They stood only a short measure taller than us, but were delicate as fine porcelain. Their heads looked like octopi, including the sack-like body behind the eyes. Around the neck, though, was a fringe of short tentacles, like an Elizabethan ruff. A bulbous body was suspended below the fringe, and from it sprouted three clusters of longer tentacles, two where the arms would be on a human, and the last descending from the base of the body. It was the eyes, though, that held our attention. Though alien, they nonetheless bore the look of a sad intelligence, as if their owners bore some heavy burden they could not shed.

The next time we dreamed we found ourselves in the forum again. The saudeleurs welcomed us as friends, and they celebrated our coming with dances and songs. At first Vicki and I merely watched, but as our dreams continued we began to join with them. The festivities then turned more solemn, as if they had become a ceremony. The saudeleurs sang our praises, hailing us as saviors. They called Vicki the mother of their god and me its father. They called upon Katoluha to bless our union and its fruits, and then they encouraged us to make love. We did so willingly, for several nights straight, and each time the saudeleurs seemed to become more ecstatic.

The dreams finally climaxed one night, when they took us to see the tomb of the being they protected. It was located at the bottom of the abyss, deep inside the submerged mountain that formed the atoll, deeper than even the saudeleurs could go. However, a tower was constructed on its top and that permitted them to commune with the being. They led us out past the edge of the shelf and over the abyss, until we reached the tower looming up out of the gloom of the depths. It was constructed of the same type of stone as the saudeleurs' city, but the blocks were colossal. It also had the same alien geometry, but this building seemed to shift and flex even as we watched it, disdaining all stability. We dived down its length, going quite deep, until we reached an opening. We swam through it into a tunnel that curved up and emerged into a chamber filled with trapped air. As I look back on it now, I realize it should have been pitch black, yet somehow I was able to see clearly.

There a group of saudeleurs waited for us. I was surprised to see them out of the water. Unlike regular octopi, they held their shape, supported by their bulbous bodies, and their thick, ropy base tentacles gave them good, if not swift, mobility. Their bodies were quite beautiful, displaying vivid phosphorescent colors that flashed and swam across their flesh, but I saw they were also finely tattooed, with intricate abstract designs intermixed with pictures of octopoid creatures.

As in previous dreams, we were greeted with song and celebration, but there was a distinct difference this time. For one thing, they sounded like chants or hymns, as if they were part of a religious ritual. I also got the feeling that it wasn't for our benefit, and we were largely ignored, except at one point where two of the saudeleurs who had brought us here guided us towards one wall. There, engraved into one of the gigantic blocks, was a bas-relief. One of the decorated saudeleurs stood before it, facing it, waving its tentacles and chanting. It was flanked by two others, chorusing with it. For some reason, I couldn't see the relief clearly, except that it looked like some kind of cephalopod, though not like any I recognized. I found that odd at the time, since I could see everything else quite clearly. Now I know why.

When the priests — for that's what they clearly were — had finished their adoration and sanctification, Vicki and I were led away to a different part of the chamber. There sat an oddly shaped table made of stone. It looked like an inverted "Y," with the mouth of the arms facing us. I was directed off to one side, while Vicki was taken right up to it. Without instruction, she lay down on it, her body on the stem and her legs spread, one on each arm. I wanted to protest, but I found I couldn't act. I wondered at that for sometime after, why we couldn't act for ourselves when in past dreams we had seemed able to do so. Now, though, thinking back on it, I realize that we may not have been acting on our own at any time, only we had never realized it before now.

The priests gathered around her and resumed their inhuman chanting. As they did so, a new priest suddenly appeared. It looked extremely old and wizened, almost mummified. It drifted up inside Vicki's spread legs, right up to her hips. It then reached into itself and pulled out a spherical glob of jelly about the size of a walnut. This it inserted into her — all the way, I imagine, up into her womb. It then stepped back, and I was taken to stand where it had stood before. Again, without being instructed, I began to *mate* with Vicki. A clinical word, but it was a clinical action: There was no emotion attached to it, no passion; it was purely mechanical. Even masturbation is accompanied by a sexual thrill, but neither of us felt anything, even when I came inside her. Afterwards I simply stepped back and waited.

The ceremony continued for some time after that, though how long I couldn't say. Eventually, the scene just sort of faded, and we awoke inside the structure, lying inside the circle of log pillars.

We looked at each other, unable to say anything, but we knew what we were thinking. I reached out tentatively and laid my hand on Vicki's stomach. She looked at me apprehensively, but I honestly didn't know what to expect. I was relieved when I felt nothing, and I told her so, but she didn't look reassured.

After that, we didn't set foot on the island again, and unfortunately we didn't make love again either. As if to accentuate that, we started dressing again. We talked of

leaving, since we no longer had a reason to stay, but Vicki didn't want to go, not until she was sure, though sure of *what*, she couldn't, or wouldn't, say. I was pretty sure, though, she meant whether what we had dreamed was real.

I tried to assure her it wasn't, that it was just a fantasy brought on by our surroundings, but I couldn't convince her. How two of us had shared the very same series of dreams, never occurred to either of us, not even at this point. Now, too late, I have to attribute it to the mind-control we had been experiencing.

Well, I really didn't want to leave either. We had paid for a full month and we had only been here for three weeks, and I saw no harm in staying for the fourth.

By the end of that week I thought we were out of the woods. Vicki seemed fine and her latest menstrual period had begun the day before. We even telephoned our parents and told them we would be leaving in another two or three days. The next day, however, her period suddenly stopped, as if someone had closed a tap — and by the end of the day she could feel a stirring inside her. The day after that I could feel it as well.

Then, starting the very next day, her belly began to swell. By the end of the day it was as the size of a basketball; by the end of the following day it was twice that size; and by noon the day after that she was as big as any woman after nine full months.

We were both terrified now and we didn't know what to do. The only thing I could think of was to get her back to Ponape, but Vicki insisted that I had to find out the truth. She urged me to try to get into the tower. What she asked made no sense, and at first I refused, but as I made preparations to get under way she went on and on about it, until finally she wore me down and I agreed to try, just to shut her up.

We set sail at dawn the next day. Thankfully she had not gotten any bigger during the night. We motored to the spire in the middle of the lagoon and I tied the boat to it. I didn't know how deep I might have to go, but luckily we had brought scuba gear with us. It wasn't much, just one tank for each of us, but I was able to con-

nect both to one regulator. Vicki lay out on the deck, since she was too big to fit comfortably in our stateroom bed. I had rigged a sunshade out of a piece of canvas for her, to give her some relief from the sun, and she had wrapped a sheet around her, now being too large for any of her clothes to fit her. I kissed her before I left; she smiled gratefully. Then I jumped overboard before I could change my mind.

Everything about the tower was exactly as it was in my dream, only worse, particularly the visual effect. Fortunately the deeper I went the darker it got, so after a short while I couldn't see much, but in the region close to the surface, where there was plenty of light, the architecture was such that not only did my mind refuse to perceive it, I suffered from some kind of mortal apprehension as well. It was all I could do to keep from screaming, throwing off my tanks, and rocketing to the surface.

According to my depth gauge I went down over 150 feet before I finally saw the opening in the beam of my flashlight. It looked more like a punched hole than an actual portal. I swam up to it and shone my lantern inside it. I wasn't sure what I expected to see, but fortunately I saw nothing except a rough-hewn tunnel going straight back into the tower. As I started to swim in, I touched the outer wall with my left hand, then jerked my hand away in alarm. The stone was so cold it burned, and my hand went numb. I exercised the fingers, trying to work some feeling back into it, but no sensation returned. I should have gone back up then and there, but I made a promise to Vicki, so I continued on, careful not to touch the sides of the tunnel.

After a fair distance the tunnel connected with a circular stair well. I looked down and saw a faint greenish glow, as if from a light far away. I was tempted to go down, but I was already almost too deep. Besides, in our dreams we went up, so up I went. I swam nearly fifty feet before I saw above me in the light beam a rippling surface. Sure enough, when I broke through I found myself in the ceremonial chamber—just like in the dreams. I played the light around to make sure the place was empty, and when I didn't see anything I clambered out. Despite their clumsy weight, I kept the tanks on in case I had to make a quick getaway. However, I spat out the mouthpiece and lifted the face mask onto my forehead to be more comfortable.

Everything was as I remembered. The Y-shaped table was against one wall and the relief was on the opposite. I went to examine it first. This time I saw it clearly, and I wish now I hadn't. It was *hideous*, but not artistically. The artistry was in fact exquisite and highly sophisticated.

No, it was the subject matter that was atrocious. I can't do justice to what I saw, and I'm not sure I should try. All I can say — all I will say — is that it reminded me of a painting by Hieronymus Bosch, not in style or execution, but in its *grotesqueness*. It was a gigantic cephalopod, but some alien nightmarish cross between an octopus, a squid, and a cuttlefish. Its eyes; my God, even now they give me the shudders just to think about them. They seemed *alive* somehow, full of malevolent, unreasoning hate, yet also arrogant cunning, and an uncanny perception, as if they could see into my soul.

I tried to move closer, but my flippers trod on something. When I looked down, I involuntarily shrieked. There, at the foot of the relief, was the body of the mummified priest, only it was truly mummified now. I backed away from it; for some reason I expected it to still be alive. But it didn't move, and it looked thoroughly desiccated, as if it had been dead for decades. Sickened, I turned around and headed back to examine the table. I had gotten only halfway, however, when I heard a noise behind me, like dry wood being dragged over bricks. I froze, terrified. I *knew* what it was, but I refused to turn around and look at it. Yet I couldn't run away either. I simply stood there, my eyes tightly shut, beseeching God to make it go away. Then a shriveled, desiccated tentacle flopped onto my shoulder and draped down my chest. I jumped away and spun around; *there in the light stood the ancient saudeleur hierophant*. It made no further attempt to approach, but simply stared at me with those sad, wise eyes. Then it spoke, not in words, but in thoughts that popped into my head. I can't remember now what it said, but I do remember how it addressed me: *Father of God*.

I'm afraid I lost it then. I screamed and I threw the lantern at it. I missed and when it hit the floor it shattered and went out, plunging me into total darkness. I started running around like a madman — at least as well as swim fins would permit me — searching for the stairwell. I crashed into walls several times before more saudeleurs came and grappled with me. I struggled as hard as I could, but there were too many of them, and despite their delicate appearance they were very strong. They bore me down, stripped off my tanks, mask, fins, and trunks, tied me up, and carried me off. They took me only a short distance, however, before dumping me into the stairwell, where more of them took hold of me and carried me down through the water.

I tried to hold my breath as long as I could, but after what seemed liked too short a while I gasped and sucked in water. Amazingly, however, I did not drown. I don't know how they did it, but they somehow made it possible for me to breathe in water. They took me deeper and deeper, and gradually my eyes adjusted to the greenish light I had seen before. How long we traveled I cannot say, but finally we emerged into a huge chamber. I realize now it was the interior of the tomb, though how we could survive the crushing pressure I still do not understand. They stopped and maneuvered me around so that I could see the floor. There I saw *IT*, the monstrous, blasphemous *Thing* that slept in safety and in secret, hidden away from mankind, tended to and worshipped by the saudeleurs. It looked like the creature in the bas-relief, but the reality was a million times worse than the depiction. It was more than I could comprehend or tolerate, and I screamed as my conscious mind shut down.

Yet my subconscious could still see It, Its cyclopean body, Its myriad tentacles, Its putrescent flesh. *And Its eyes* — half-lidded, drowsy, languid with torpor, but blazing with an intense unquenchable unforgiving hatred of me and mankind and all we represented. I could feel Its hate as it washed over me, and Its jealousy, and Its agony. It wanted to be free of its prison of moribund slumber; It wanted to reclaim Its ownership of this planet, the sovereignty we usurped; It wanted once more to stride across the face of the Earth, to worship its god and master, Katoluha, and to sing the praises of His masters, the Old Ones, and of *their* masters, the Outer Gods. Those eyes bore into my brain as my mind retreated from them, and finally I lost all consciousness as I slipped into blissful oblivion.

When I awoke it was night. I lay on the beach of the largest island, with Vicki beside me, cradling me in her arms. We were both completely naked. In the distance I saw something burning, and with a sense of resigned dread I knew it was the boat. We watched it helplessly until the gas tanks exploded and it sank from sight. Then we buried our heads in each others arms and cried hysterically. Eventually we exhausted ourselves and fell into a stuporous sleep.

I had thought that was the end, but it wasn't. Over the next two weeks Vicki's womb continued to expand, but in spurts. She would grow for a day and then nothing would happen for two or three. Each time it happened, she was wracked by severe pains and debilitating fevers, so that the only relief she received was to lie in the lagoon. At those times I would float with her, hold her to me, try to comfort her, but she was unaware of me at those times. After each growth spurt, she would crawl — she could no longer walk — back up the beach to the makeshift lean-to I had constructed. There she would collapse, to rest and wait for the next cycle. Each time, her mind faded a little more. She soon was no longer a

woman but a child, and she became more childlike with each passing day. She still seemed to know me, but I had become more like a parent than a husband.

The morning after the saudeleurs had destroyed the boat, I found that they had first salvaged from it things they thought we would need. There, scattered along the beach, was all the food we had left (though the refrigerated stuff would spoil in another day), blankets, a shovel, a couple of kitchen knives including a huge carving knife, and the fresh water, among other miscellaneous useless items. What was really surprising was that they had also salvaged the motor fuel canisters; why they thought we would need them I still cannot guess. And one day I found among some junk the flare pistol we kept on board for emergencies. It was still sealed in its watertight case along with three flares. It was useless as a weapon, but it comforted me to keep it handy. In my desperation I imagined that a plane might fly over and I could signal it, but of course none ever did.

During those two weeks the saudeleurs would come each day, to feed Vicki special foods (which she greedily devoured as if starving), to give praise to her and the Thing growing inside her, and to instruct me. (All this seemed as extravagant as our previous dreams, but it seemed to be real this time, whatever that means.) Apparently they expected me to teach the Thing all it needed to know, which was everything written on the tablets in the structure. They didn't explain why they could not do it themselves, but I got the impression that as the "Father of the God" it was my responsibility, and according to some taboo no one else could do it. So they taught me to read them. With my knowledge of Polynesian I learned quickly, and soon I was able to read the tablets without their aid. That's how I learned what the Thing inside my wife was and was meant to be, and why we had been chosen to be Its foster parents.

The saudeleurs were desperate; they were dying, and with the Being they worshipped and guarded still entombed, there could be no more of them. Before It fell into Its deathlike sleep, however, It entrusted to them a certain number of Its eggs. With these, they could grow an avatar, and It could then make more of

them. The problem was, the egg had to be incubated in the womb of a fertile woman who nonetheless had borne no children, and it had to be fertilized by a man who loved the woman and wanted to beget children on her. In the past they had tried with Polynesians here on Ponape and elsewhere, but for one reason or another they always failed: either the people were infertile, or the women had already borne children, or they had no men who loved them, or they had lost the capacity to love, or their neighbors would attack them and kill the "parents" to prevent the birth of the avatars. Now there were only a few eggs left. To them our coming must have seemed a miracle; we were perfect for them, being married and fertile but childless. But we were not devotees of their religion, so using us was risky. We might not have been controllable; we might have been able to resist their influence, their spells and rituals; we might even have been willing to destroy ourselves rather than permit the avatar to be born. But when they discovered the depth of our passion for each other, they decided to take a gamble, and so they took advantage of our weaknesses — our desire for a child and our lust for one another — to gain control over our wills.

And it had worked. Their avatar was developing well; in another week It would be mature enough to break out of what was left of Vicki's body, and then after It had learned everything I was to teach It, It would take Its place as their conscious god. It would make more of them, and they would spread throughout the Pacific, carrying the worship of their god with them, and thus Its influence would spread, until It controlled the whole of this region of the world. With their aid, It and the saudeleurs could then work for the day when the stars would once again be right and Katoluha and His brethren would be free to once again walk the earth.

I have resolved not to let that happen. Unfortunately there is only one way to stop them. I am loath to do it, but I have no other choice. The saudeleurs don't think I can do it, because of my love for Vicki, but they do not understand, cannot understand, that it is because I love her that I not only can, but *must* do it. And I also know just *how* to do it. They have provided me with the means, though they are unaware of this.

It has taken me a week to prepare, in secret, trying to keep it all hidden from them. Fortunately, they were not suspicious of my activities; they probably thought I was just doing simple domestic chores in any event. But I am now ready; all I need is to wait for the right moment. Vicki is now incredibly huge. She lies in the lagoon all the time, to support her weight and cool her fevers, her head just barely above water, but she couldn't move in any event because her arms and legs have completely disappeared except for her hands and feet. The sight of her once wondrous body, now bloated and oblong, looking like an obscene seal, fills me with misery for myself, heartache for her, and rage for them. Now that I am finished I stay with her as often as I can, and though her mind is virtually gone, she looks at me with such desperate longing, her anguished expression begging me wordlessly to end her torment. But I have to wait. The Thing inside her has stretched her skin so tightly it is translucent, and I can see It dimly. It is now aware of Itself and Its surroundings, though not quite ready yet to emerge. I can see It watching me, with Its octopus eyes; I know It can see me, and I know It knows what I am thinking. So I have to wait until It sleeps again, when It will undergo its final growth and change, when It will finally break free after It awakens for the last time. I very nearly ran out of time, but I made it and I am ready. I need only be patient a little while longer.

I t is done. That was the hardest task I have ever had to perform, but now that it is accomplished I am glad of it.

The Thing fell asleep just before dusk. I waited to make sure It was completely unconscious, then tied a makeshift pulley system I had carved out of dead wood to a tree, fed the rope I made out of vines through it, and tied it around Vicki's chest. I then uncovered the pit I had dug and slowly dragged her body out of the water, up the beach, and into the pit. All the time I was worried that they would discover what I was doing, or that the Thing would awaken, but God (the Christian God, not their profane, monstrous, alien "god") was kind to me and I was not interrupted. Once Vicki was in the pit, I ran to fetch the gas containers and carried them back. I then opened them and poured some of the fuel into the pit and over the grotesque cocoon.

I retrieved the flare gun, loaded one of the three flares into it, and stood at the edge, looking down at her. In the waning light of day I could see her face clearly. She looked up at me and for the first time in days she smiled. Her features relaxed into a look of serenity and she closed her eyes. I lifted the pistol and took aim; I cocked the hammer and began to squeeze the trigger. It all happened so slowly that at first I thought nothing was going to happen, but then the gun fired unexpectedly, and I saw her head explode in an burst of flame. I cried out then, shrieking my emotional release in a wail of despair. When I calmed down enough to stop shaking, I loaded the second flare and fired it into the pit, igniting the fuel.

The Thing's eyes suddenly snapped open. It gazed at

me in pure hate and began crying out in alarm and fear, broadcasting an ululation like a siren. I went mad. Shrieking again, this time in fury, I loaded the last flare, turned the gun on It, and fired directly into Its eyes. I kept pulling the trigger for some moments after that, until my mind cleared, then I threw the gun into the pit. The cry intensified, and I could see the Thing struggling to break out. As I watched in horror, the skin stretched tighter and began to tear. My mind almost gone with terror, I poured the remaining fuel into the pit, then retreated from the conflagration, collapsing into the sand. I watched numbly as tentacles ripped free and flailed about in the night, but they were ablaze, and rapidly the cry died away as the flames consumed It along with what was left of my beloved Victoria.

How long I lay where I fell I do not know, but when next I was aware I saw it was morning. Soon they would come to preside over Its release. I had to get this manuscript finished before then, because I knew that, no longer being of any use to them, I would not escape punishment for this desecration. So I forced myself to my feet and returned to the bungalow.

I can hear them coming for me now. They've found the pit and the charred remains, and they have sounded their unearthly lament and beat their bodies in frustrated anguish. Now they advance on the bungalow. I have just enough time to jot down a few last sentences and hide the manuscript away before they reach me. I won't make it easy for them. I'll run into the jungle, to the structure in the clearing; I've made weapons, set traps. I will kill as many of them as I can today, God willing, before they take me. I don't know what they will do to me, but I am not afraid. Soon I will be with Vicki in Paradise, and together we will walk in the garden of the Lord forever.

Editor's Note: The manuscript ends at this point. The investigators found very little to corroborate this account; certainly no bodies or fire pit was discovered, and no trace of the remaining supplies or the boat could be found. However, the team did find the structures spoken of, including the tower. The US government, in conjunction with the Japanese and the Pohnpeians, has decided to sponsor a group of archaeologists to investigate these structures, and look for any sign of the so-called saudeleurs. As of this writing, they have persuaded the famous husband and wife team of Hector and Wilemena Sorenson to lead the expedition.

BLOOD MAIDENS
(CASTLE CSEJTHE, SLOVAKIA)

There is a wailing on the wind tonight
Akin to maidens' voices mad with pain,
Immortal echoes of too mortal fright,
Lost innocence drained dry.
What husks remain?
Only those few which wolves or winter spared.
The rest drift disembodied through this hell
Whose tortures scores of maids & peasants shared
Before the laggard fist of justice fell.

At times one strain shrills high above the rest,
Some thrice-damned soul forever crying out
Its torment.
So the Countess greets her guests:
Noblesse oblige beyond a scrap of doubt
From bricked-up rooms she haunts eternally . . .
Cursed not with solitude, but company.

— *Ann K. Schwader*

BY KEVIN L. O'BRIEN

PETROGLYPHS

by Richard A. Lupoff

illustrated by David Grilla

"You gotta make up your mind, Delbert. Do you want to be an office boy and printer's devil all your life and make coffee fer other men, or do you want to make something of yerself?"

The paper was put to bed. She'd be coming off the press in a little while. Edgardo Carrero, our pressman, was giving the press its third or fourth check-up. Nothing escaped his eye and I guess it was all that checking and rechecking that kept the *Sentinel* on her schedule. Every Friday morning, regular as clockwork, there was the *Sentinel* on the street, getting people upset.

Bill van Hopkins, founder, editor, and publisher of the Sour Creek *Sentinel* had his feet up on his desk and a coffee cup full of bourbon in his hand.

"You know I want to be a newsman, Bill."

"Mr. van Hopkins."

"Sorry. Mr. van Hopkins."

Bill took a deep swig of his bourbon. I figured, another refill or so and he wouldn't mind my calling him by his first name. It was a ritual, every Thursday night.

"How old are you, son?"

"Fifteen," I told him.

He squinted at me over the edge of his coffee cup. His cheeks were bright red and his hair was falling over his forehead. He needed a haircut.

"Fifteen, eh? You don't look it to me. You sure you're that old?"

"Yes, sir."

"Where you from, son? Your name's Delbert, ain't it? Delbert Marston?"

"Yes, sir. You know me, Mr. van Hopkins, sir. I was born right here in Sour Creek."

"Call me Bill, son. No need to be formal around here."

"Yes, sir."

"You want a sip of this here coffee, Delbert?" He didn't wait for me to answer. He picked up another coffee cup and poured a couple of fingers of bourbon. He handed me the cup and I took a very small sip.

I really am fifteen, or pretty close to it anyhow, but I'm short for my age and kind of skinny, and I don't like liquor much. I know who my mother is and I see her around town once in a while and I'm always polite to her. I don't know for sure who my father was. My ma'am says he got murdered before I was born. She calls herself Mrs. Marston, so I guess my pap was Mr. Marston. Ma'am says he was a Major in the Confederate Army and he came home from the war and married her and got me started in her and then he went out one night and got hisself murdered.

That's a good enough story for me.

"Well, son, you falling asleep or which?" Bill van Hopkins asked reached over and kicked me, but not hard. I said, "No, I ain't asleep. Did you ask me something?"

"I was going to but you fell asleep, you damned lazy wretch."

I know he didn't mean that, it's just his way of showing affection. "What were you gonna ask me, Bill?"

"Do you feel like covering a story, Delbert, that's what I was gonna ask you. You don't do nothing useful here in the office except get in the way. So how's about you going out and doing some reporting and earn your salary for once in your good for nothing life."

I put my coffee cup down and got to my feet and stood to attention the way my pap must have done in the war. I said, "Here am I, Lord, send me."

Edgardo Carrero must have been satisfied with the condition of the press because he started her up and he was working her slow and steady, the way he done every week, every Thursday night. *Ker-whumpa-ker-whumpa-ker-whumpa.*

"What's the story?" I asked Bill. "Ain't heard of no hangings coming up, no gunfights, no buildings burning down."

"Delbert, there's a big opening of that new Gilbert and Sullivan show over to the Superba Opera House this weekend. Miss Billie Benton herself is goin' to be in it, playing some kinda Japanese geechee girl or something."

I must have drooped a little but I figured, this was my first break from being an office boy and printer's devil, if I did a good job I'd get more reporting work and less making coffee for the boss.

So I said, "I'll do a great job, Bill, you can count on me.

I'll get over to the Superba and interview Miss Benton and write up the show, too."

"No you won't."

"I won't?"

"Jabber's handling the opera show."

Jabber is Walter Jabbert. He's the *Sentinel's* ace reporter. He has a notorious eye for female flesh and I could have guessed that he'd nab off the assignment of meeting Miss Billie Benton. He'll probably offer to buy her dinner and a drink while he's at it. I know he was after my ma'am at one time, but I put the kibosh on that scheme of his. He's got me by sixty pounds and half a foot, but he's slow on his feet and he don't take a wallop on the chin too good.

We're friends, now that he knows what's what.

"Okay, Bill. Jabber goes to the opera. Where do I go? Courthouse open tomorrow? Got some good case to handle?"

"Nothing like that. We got a professor about to descend upon our humble little town. One Professor F. L. Grey, of the great University of Springfield. Imagine, traveling thousands of miles just to come to Sour Creek."

"What's he coming here for? Hardly no books in this town, and not a single statue."

"Nope."

The press was going faster now. *Ker-whumpa-ker-whumpa.* Once he gets going, Mr. Carrero gets a look in his eyes and nobody better go anywhere near him.

"Couple of paintings in the saloon, though," I said. "Think he wants to look at them?"

Bill laughed. "You're gettin' warm, Delbert. Gettin' warm. Professor Grey wants to look at the rock pitchers out near the butte."

"What's he need me for, then?"

"Needs a guide, mainly. He's coming on the stage tomorrow morning. He'll check into the Lee's Arms and then you help him rent a horse from Shipley's and you ride out to the butte with him and show him the pitchers."

"That's all?"

"Make a story out of it, son. You do a good job, you might could get a real nice story out of it. Do that, you get more. You foul this up, it's back to making coffee for you."

"What if he wants to know about the pitchers?"

"Know what?"

I shrugged. Bill was refilling his coffee cup. He held the bottle of bourbon toward me until he saw that my cup was nowhere near empty. "Call yourself a writer?" he grumbled.

Then, "What if Professor Grey wants to know something about the pitchers? I don't know nothing about 'em. Nobody much does."

"Ah," Bill said, letting the word out slow and satisfied sounding. "You tell him anything you feel like. That way you'll get to be a famous scholar and Professor Grey will sit you in his book. Make you an important figger, getting sitted in a book by a professor."

"But I don't know nothing about the rock pitchers," I insisted.

Bill shook his head from side to side, a sad expression on his face like when you try real hard to explain something to some poor simple soul, and the simpleton just don't understand what you told him.

"Delbert," Bill said, "don't nobody hereabouts know nothing about them pitchers 'cept Crippled John Smith the Navajo. And he ain't no newspaper reporter, so you'll just have to make it all up. That's all. This professor don't know no better or he wouldn't have to ask. So you just make up a good story for the professor and he'll be happy and go back to Springfield and write his book, and you'll be happy and you'll come back here to the *Sentinel* and write your own story and I'll be happy. And you want me to be happy, don't you?"

I said, "I sure do, Bill." I kept my thoughts to myself, but I was thinking that Crippled John Smith was no more no Navajo than the man in the moon, he just claimed he was Navajo and got people to buy him drinks by telling 'em wild stories about the old days.

Ker-whumpa-ker-whumpa-ker-whumpa. Mr. Carrero was going away at it at the printing press like a love-crazed stallion going at it with a willing and eager mare. I was pretty tired but Bill van Hopkins was pretty obvious getting into one of his philosophical moods and in no hurry to go home to Mrs. van Hopkins. And even if he did, there was no point in my crawling into my sleeping bag in the back of the office and trying to get any shut-eye, not until Mr. Carrero finished his work and locked up and went home.

Ker-whumpa-ker-whumpa-ker-whumpa.

I went over and picked up a copy of the *Sentinel* for Bill van Hopkins and one for myself and we sat in neighborly silence (except for the continuous thumping of the press) sipping our bourbon and reading the *Sentinel*. We always print the paper on Thursday night but it's dated the next day and I always give me the creeps to think that I'm reading a newspaper out of the future.

Finally Mr. Carrero finished. A creepy silence fell over the *Sentinel* office. It was one of those moments. Some folks say that an angel must have just flew over. Some folks say it means that somebody just walked on your grave. Anyway, it was real, real quiet in the *Sentinel* office.

Then Bill van Hopkins said, "Ladies and gentlemen, it is time for all good souls to seek their nightly repast. And so, I bid you, *bon jewels*." He downed the last of his bourbon, pushed himself to his feet, and clamped his hat on his head."

Mr. Carrero took the hint. He took off his apron, hung it on its hook, and headed for the door. Mr. van Hopkins waited for him to step outside, then he followed him. He turned around and stuck his head back inside the office.

"Bright and early, Delbert," you have work to do in the morning." He meant, delivering *Sentinels*. My favorite part of my job.

Just joshing.

It was getting dark so I lit a kerosene lantern and climbed into my sleeping bag with a dime novel. Reading about detectives in the big cities back east always helps me to sleep and gives me good dreams. I need that. Otherwise I have other dreams that I don't like, and I wake up shaking and crying. Nobody gets to see me like that. Nobody. That would never do.

In the morning I went over to the saloon for breakfast. I figured there would be a few customers who'd stayed over sleeping in with the girls—they charge extra for that but if the customer is willing to pay they're happy to take his money.

A couple of cowboys were drinking at a table. I couldn't tell whether they were getting an early start on the day or had simply forgot to quit last night. I recognized 'em and we said Good morning to each other.

Then I went up to the bar to get some breakfast and would you guess who was there to serve booze and fry food. No, don't guess, I might as well just tell you. It was my mother.

She smiled at me and said, "Good morning, Delbert. How are you today?"

I said, "Hungry, ma'am."

She said, "Well, how about some nice bacon and eggs? I can fry some up for you in a jiffy. How about a piece of hard roll and a cup of coffee while you wait?"

I couldn't believe it. Butter wouldn't melt in that woman's mouth. I think the only reason I don't quit this town and start over is I'm too stubborn to let her know she's beat me, and the only reason she won't leave town is cause she don't want me to have the satisfaction of seeing the hind of her.

But the coffee was hot and the breakfast was good and I was still the first one at the *Sentinel* office to start distributing newspapers. After we finished that chore it was back to the office and sit down and address the out-of-town subscriber copies. You'd be amazed at how many people want to get the *Sour Creek Sentinel*. We have subscribers in Mexico, China, and Jerusalem. Can you imagine what some bearded old Hebrew in Jerusalem thinks about weddings and funerals and hangings in Sour Creek, Arizona Territory, You Ess of Ay? And why is he interested?

The stage arrived at noon and I met it and introduced myself to Professor Grey. The Professor was a woman—no joke! It took me a while to figure that out. She was taller than I was by four-five inches easy, and she dressed like a man and she had her hair pushed up under a broad-brimmed Stetson. Had a mighty handshake, too, and she didn't act or talk girly-girly, but she was still a woman. I guess anybody can be a professor nowadays.

Her name was Professor Frances Loretta Grey and she said she answered to Frances or Frankie but she preferred Frankie and got deef whenever anybody tried to call her Lottie.

I told her my name was Delbert and I didn't have no other preferences so she might as well just call me that and she said okay she would.

She didn't have near as much luggage as I'd have expected of a woman, neither. Just a couple of carpetbags and a box that she said had her *ee*-quipment in it. I asked her what *ee*-quipment that was and she said it was her scientific *ee*-quipment and it was fragile and had chemicals in it so would I *please* be very careful with it and I said, Well, of course, what do think I'd do, roll it like a hoop? And she got annoyed and said she just wanted to make sure it was properly cared for and I said, But of course, Your Professorship, Madame, thou needst not fear that thy <u>ee</u>-quipment will be properly cared for.

I took her over to Shipley's Hotel and Livery and saw to it that she had a nice room and asked her when she wanted to go look at the rock pitchers and she said right away if she could just get "a bite to eat" first.

So I took her over to the saloon, which was starting to fill up mainly with cowboys in for a drink or a quick nooner with the ladies. My ma'am was still on duty so I introduced Professor Frances Loretta Grey to her and my ma'am extended her hand and said, "Pleased to meetcha, Lottie," which I knew at once did not bode well for their forming no intimate bosomhood together.

Frankie and me each had a sandwich and then we walked back to Shipley's and rented her a horse and I got on my horse and we headed out to look at the rock pitchers. All Frankie took with her was a pad of some kind of thin paper, about a quarter as thick as newsprint, and some soft pencils. She said she'd have to rent a wagon and bring her *ee*-quipment out with her some

other time.

We rode for a couple of hours to the rock caves and went in and Frankie stopped and stared at the pitchers for about three weeks time, it seemed like, maybe ten minutes actual, without saying nothing. Then she said, "These are wonderful, they're just wonderful."

She took out her paper and pencils and leaned against the pitchers and started scrabbling a soft pencil back and forth on the pitcher. It might of looked strange to me, what she was doing, except we used to do it when I was a kid. If anybody had a penny we'd put a piece of paper on top of it and scrabble a pencil back and forth and you could make a nice copy of the penny that way.

Frankie Professor Frances Loretta Don't Call Me Lottie Grey was doin' exactly that making copies of the rock pitchers.

After a little I got bored watching her and went for a walk, saw a couple of interesting snakes and some nice lizards and a couple of eagles out hunting for rabbits but I didn't see no rabbits so good luck to them eagles.

We went back to Sour Creek and Frankie went upstairs at Shipley's to freshen up and invited me to have dinner with her on her *expense account*. I asked her what that was and she explained it to me. I thought that was the best idea I'd heard of in a long time and decided I'd ask Mr. Bill van Hopkins to let me have one of them things, too. Frankie said she wished me luck and I thought about them eagles looking for rabbits where there wasn't no rabbits around.

Fat chance.

But I could always try.

I had a little notebook with me and a pencil and I asked Frankie about what it was like being a professor and why she was interested in the rock pitchers and what she was going to do when she got back to the University of Springfield and made copious notes about her answers.

The next morning we started off bright and early. Frankie had returned Shipley's horse all safe and sound and rented a wagon and a horse to pull it. I carried her box down from her room and loaded it onto the wagon and we headed for the caves again.

Frankie said we had a lot of work to do so we took a couple of jugs of water and some sandwiches with us. She was wearing her big Stetson, which was smart even for a professor from the University of Springfield. Not as smart as me, of course. I wore a straw hat. Just as good for protecting from the sun and a lot lighter, but even so, she didn't do so bad. She wore canvas britches and a plaid shirt and she didn't look too bad at that. Certainly a hell of a lot different from my ma'am or any of the girls that work at the saloon.

We got to the caves and I tethered the horse and lifted the box down off the wagon. I was doing a lot of work for Professor Frances Loretta Grey and not getting paid for it, just my salary from the *Sentinel* plus I figured I was getting some meals paid for off Professor Grey's *expense account*.

I guess by now those cave pitchers are pretty famous and everybody knows what they look like, but then hardly nobody knew about them except the kids from Sour Creek. We used to go out to the caves when we weren't working or at school and look at the cave pitchers. When I was a little kid we used to go out there and make up stories about the cave pitchers, we decided they was made by old people a long time ago, not the Navajos or anybody like that but people who lived here longer ago than the Navajos and made those pitchers before they left or when they knew they was going to die or something. We made up scary stories.

Once we decided to have a contest. Everybody put in a penny and anybody who was brave enough to stay in the cave with the pitchers overnight would win the prize. My friend Danny Wilson said he was the bravest kid in Sour Creek and he'd be the first to stay in the cave overnight and win the prize.

We all went out there and had a meeting and swapped stories and we left Danny with a bag of sandwiches and a canteen and everybody went home. We went back out there the next morning and Danny was gone and so was the bag of sandwiches and the canteen and we never saw him again so everybody took back his penny except we didn't know what to do with the extra penny so we went to Danny's ma'am and gave it to her to keep for him.

The Professor's *ee*-quipment was a photograph camera and photograph plates and chemicals for developing the photographs. She set up her camera and said she was going to take photographs of the rock pitchers. To take each photograph she would put a plate in her photograph camera and pull out a slide and then we would just wait and wait for the photograph to get took.

She said she could work faster if she had more light but it wasn't very light in the caves so she had to make a longer exposure. I said, Oh, sure, ever'body knows about longer exposures and shorter exposures. I don't think the Professor believed me because she laughed but she didn't say nothing to challenge me.

While she was taking her photographs of the rock pitchers she asked me questions about the pitchers but I couldn't tell her much because nobody really knew who made them or when or why. I told her about our meetings when I was a kid and when I told her about Danny Wilson she got excited and wanted to know more about him but all I could tell her was that he disappeared and his ma'am was really upset when we told her about it and after a while she left town.

I wish my ma'am would do the same.

We was taking a break for lunch when Crippled John Smith the Navajo come upon us. I won't say he was no sneak but he was leading his horse and walking, not riding, which he was able to do quieter that way so he arrived and we didn't know he was there until the cave got darker than it was already. We was eating our lunch in the cave, Frankie and me, because it was cool in there out of the sunlight, and without no warning the light got mostly cut off and we looked and there was Crippled John Smith standing in the mouth of the cave looking at us.

Frankie Grey took me by the elbow and leaned over and hissed into my ear, "Who is that man?"

I said, "That's just Crippled John Smith."

"Is he dangerous?" Frankie asked me.

I said, "No. He's a little bit crazy but he don't do nobody no harm."

Crippled John Smith took a couple of steps inside the cave so he wasn't blocking the mouth no more and the light got a little better. Professor Grey's photograph camera was standing there pointed at one of the rock pitchers. She stood between the photograph camera and Crippled John Smith. I thought she was going to say something to him but he spoke first.

"What are you doing?"

Professor Grey said, "I'm investigating these petroglyphs."

That was a new word to me but I figured Professor Grey was talking about the rock pitchers and either Crippled John Smith knew what it meant or else he just didn't care to stop and ask.

What he did, though, was talk the way he did in Sour Creek, that made everybody know he was crazy. He started his crazy talk, which sounded to me like a combination of regular words mixed up with some Chinee or Japanee words and some Hebrew and some Latin that I once heard a Jewish rabbi and a Popish priest talk when they came through Sour Creek on the stage on their way to Seattle or someplace.

Crippled John Smith can talk regular, and when you ask him about the crazy talk he says he's talking Navajo, but a couple real Navajos came through Sour Creek one time and I remember Crippled John Smith tried talking his crazy talk to them and they didn't understand him at all. They just shook their heads. They could talk a little regular and they said he wasn't no Navajo, he was just a crazy man.

Which I believe is the truth.

The rock pitchers, well, I ain't going to describe 'em much because Professor Grey's photographs been all over the world by now, including in a special roady graver supplement to the Sour Creek *Sentinel*. We even got extra copies down to the *Sentinel* office. If you want one just come by and lay out your scratch and your wish shall be our command. If I ain't there Mr. Bill van Hopkins or Mr. Walter Jabbert or even Mr. Edgardo Carrero will sell you one. Or if you don't live hereabouts you can even send in the price by mail and I will personally address a copy of the supplement myself and make certain that it goes out to you safe and sound.

But for the moment, the rock pitchers showed some really strange galoots in what look like deep sea divers' outfits like in those stories Mr. Verne writes over in France, Europe. You know, they're wearing heavy boots and baggy suits and what look like helmets on their heads with little winders in front to look out of. And if you can make 'em out, you can look *in* the winders and see their faces a little.

But I think the artist wasn't very good at his work. Heck, I can draw better-looking people than them and I ain't never been to artist school. Or maybe he was just cock-eyed. I mean, those folks look so tall and skinny, they must be 'leven feet tall. You can tell because the artist he put a couple regular size people in the pitchers too, so you can tell.

And their faces ain't no Money Listers neither. He got their eyes all messed up, weird and slanty like a Chineeman only lots bigger and black and shiny.

Also the artist he put some kind of crazy boats in the pitchers, too. You know what they look like? You read that crazy book by Mr. Verne about some Captain name of Nemo? You remember that boat he had that went under the ocean? Well, these boats in the rock pitchers look like that.

Submarines, they're called. You could look it up in Mr. Webster's dictionary.

Crippled John Smith says they ain't no submarines, and for once he made sense to me cause there ain't no ocean for a submarine to *go* under in Arizona Territory.

Crazy.

You know Sergeant McWhorter?

Town like Sour Creek has plenty of strange characters in it. Sergeant McWhorter, he's an old-timer. Says he was just a boy back in 1860, wound up in the army dur-

ing the late unpleasantness of that time.

One time I was eating breakfast down to the saloon and Sergeant McWhorter must have been lonely cause he came over and started up a conversation. He wanted to talk about the late unpleasantness and I figgered just to be polite I'd let him rare back and have at it. I even encouraged him by asking him which side he fit on and he said, both sides.

I said, How was that, wasn't you either a Union or a Reb? And you know what he said? I'll tell you what he said.

He said, and I remember his exact words, swear it on a Bible, his exact words, he said, "I useta be twins. Always fit with my brother. Couldn't agree with him about nothing. I said a apple was green, he'd say it was yaller. I said a dog was yaller, he'd say it was off-white. Now I ask you, what in the world is a off-white dog? A dog is white or it ain't white, it ain't off-white, no more'n an apple is a off-apple or a horse is a off-horse."

See, George McWhorter, he rambles.

So I got him back on the track and he says, "The war broke out and my brother says, 'I'm going out and enlist,' and I said, 'Which side you figger to enlist *on*?' and he told me, so of course I had to go out and enlist on t'other side."

George looks at my plate, I got half a sandwich left of what I was eating, he says, "You gonna finish that?" and I says, "Dunno, ain't decided yet," and he says, "Here, son, I'll save you the trouble," and he reaches and takes my half a sandwich and eats it up every bit before I have a chance to stop him.

Anyhow, I showed him one of Professor Grey's photographs of the rock pitchers and asked him what he thought of them and he looked at the submarine and he said, yep, it surely was a submarine, they had 'em in the late unpleasantness, the Rebs they had one called the *Hunley* and Union side had one called the *Intelligent Whale* and another one that they bought from France, Europe, called the *Alligator*.

I asked him once again which side he fit on and he said, real sad, real real sad, that his brother fit on one side and he fit on t'other and he got kilt dead so his brother had to take over and be both twins, and that was him, now. It wasn't him sitting there in the saloon, my own ma'am watching us disapproving, it was his brother.

But meanwhile I guess I got away from my story because there was Professor Grey and Crippled John Smith and me standing there in the cave looking at the rock pitchers and Professor Grey taking her photographs and all of a sudden Crippled John Smith says, "They're a-coming back. They're a-coming back. The old people went away and they forgot me, the sonsabitches, they forgot to take me with them, so they're coming back and they'd better take me with them this time."

He was talking regular, see? None of that crazy German-Russian-Greek stuff that he called Navajo. He said, "You two git on back to town because you ain't from the old people and they'll kill you dead they find you here but they'll take me with 'em this time or I'll know the reason why!"

He was really, really, angry. I'd use a different term to tell you how angry he was, but that wouldn't be polite. So I'll just say, he was really, really, *really* angry.

So Professor Grey and me, we figured we'd pack up and head back into Sour Creek for the night, and we did. She went to her room at Shipley's to "powder her nose and freshen up a bit," as she said it, and we met later and had a good drink together and dinner. And Cripple John Smith stayed out there at the caves.

Professor Grey and me went back out there the next morning and there was no sign of Cripple John Smith, we figgered he'd got cold in the night and headed back into Sour Creek, but when we got back to Sour Creek nobody said they'd seen him. And nobody ever did see him again.

Maybe the old people came back for him in their submarine.

I wrote up the whole thing and for the Sour Creek *Sentinel* and Mr. Bill van Hopkins liked it so much he gave me a fifteen cent bonus. (P)

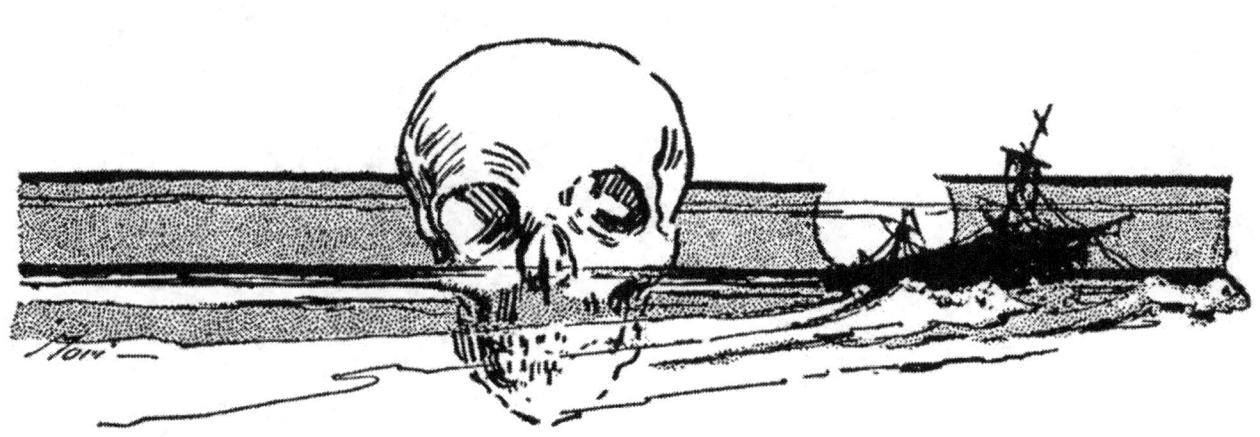

LEMURIA

Some lost continents are more "lost" than others. Scholars debate whether Plato was referring to a genuine tradition of an island civilization of Atlantis. If he was not simply spinning an allegory like Thomas More's *Utopia* (the name of which combines the Greek words for "good place," *eu-topia*, and "no place," *ou-topia*!), what was he referring to? Some think he had in mind the Island of Thera, others Minoan Crete. But even more lost is the Lost Continent of Lemuria where many pulp stories and novels are set, including Lin Carter's Thongor of Lemuria books, Stanton Coblentz's "Enchantress of Lemuria," and E. Charles Vivian's *City of Wonder*. Sinbad the Sailor visits the remains of Lemuria in the movie *Golden Voyage of Sindbad*. But it never existed, any more than Thongor or Sinbad did.

Scientists first postulated the existence of "Lemuria" as a long-gone land bridge connecting India and Madagascar (and this located in the Indian, not the Pacific, Ocean, contra those who would identify Lemuria with Mu, James Churchward's lost continent which never existed either). You see, they needed it in order to explain the presence of closely related species of lemurs in South India and on Madagascar. Once upon a time, scientists posited, the lemurs must have been able to walk the distance. But Lemuria became obsolete with the rise of Continental Drift theory. Once scientists realized that the continents had once been connected, that explained how similar animals could now be found in far-flung places. Originally, they had not been flung at all, much less far.

But before Lemuria was canceled as a superfluous hypothesis, Madame Blavatsky and her scribe W. Scott-Elliot (*The Lost Lemuria*) had adopted the dubious landmass into their colorful cosmology. The Theosophical Society proclaimed Lemuria the home of one of the primordial "Root-Races" of mankind, and from these speculations Robert E. Howard derived his own fictional Lemuria, stomping ground of the shambling apemen who preceded the clean-limbed Atlanteans of whom King Kull was the scion.

—Stanley C. Sargent

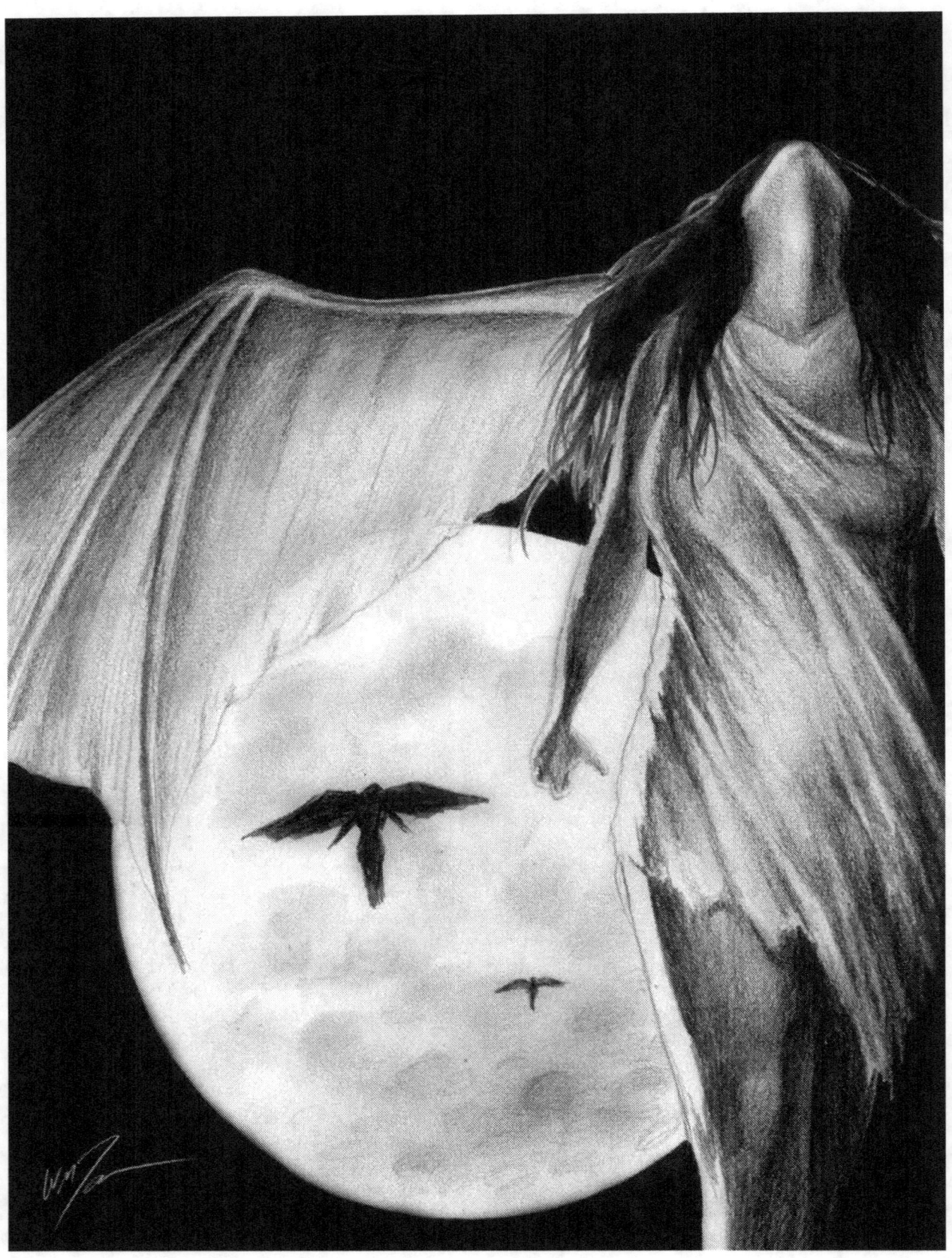

THE THIRD SISTER

by Andrew Kelly

Soaring over a hot, shimmering desert toward ancient ruins on the horizon. No sense of time, or place. Memories so old as to be forgotten. Or just buried deep.

Arcing and descending, swooping low over rocky hills; shadow, dark wings extended, cast against the bone-white stone. A sense of others nearby, not visible, but close. Close…

Oh Jesus, Dennis thought; his first impulse was to slam the handset back on the cradle. "What is it, Aimee?" he said, resigned.

"Hey, Den, good to hear your voice again."

"Aimee…"

"C'mon Den, I've been good. Haven't bothered you in ages."

"Do I have to get an unlisted number?"

"I'm having the dreams again, Dennis. Really vivid and intense. Like visions. You're the only one I can talk to—"

"What about your shrink, Aimee? She gets paid to listen to this crap. I don't."

"You're the only one who understands—"

"I understand nuisance calls. I thought you understood that it's over—"

"Ah, well, yes. Modern relationships. Just jump ship when the waters get a little choppy. So much for commitment."

"You're the one who needs commitment."

"Funny. Funny man. Dennis, *please.* It's really bad. *Bad.* It wasn't when we were together. I thought you cared."

"Aimee, listen. Don't contact me again, in any way. Ever. Understand? I mean it. You hear me?"

"Yes."

"Goodbye, Aimee."

"Dennis?"

Pam sighed. "It's really eating at you, isn't it? She's harmless, right? We're not talking Psycho Stalker Bitch from Hell, are we?"

Dennis sat next to her on the couch and picked up the TV remote control. "She's as harmless as any ditzy New Age freak can be."

"I feel sorry for her."

"You didn't live with her for a year. That emotionally fragile vulnerability gets old real quick. She was obsessed with past lives and astral projection. Her weird dreams were icing on the cake."

"Flying dreams, weren't they?" Pam smiled. "Aren't they supposed to be sexual?"

Dennis mechanically pressed the channel button; images flashed across the TV screen in a strobing blur. "Nothing sexy about hers. She called them out of body experiences. Imagined herself as some giant bird of prey. Feelings of great rage and anger as she soared, searching. Hunting."

Pam frowned. "Repressed hostility. I can relate to that." She leaned close to him. "You have to learn to treat your women better."

He yawned. "Another harpy. Why do I always attract the crazy ones?"

That earned him an elbow in the ribs.

"Aimee, you're not going to do anything stupid, are you?"

"Like this call?"

"I'm serious. Talk to your doctor. Take your meds. You sound a bit disassociated."

"I'm flying more frequently, Den. Toward some goal or destination."

Dennis rolled his eyes and cursed himself for not hanging up.

"It's not astral projection," she continued, "I was wrong about that. I'm in another form. Animus, perhaps, or transmogrification, or my animal totem."

He was silent for a moment. He'd been furious when she called again. What bothered him was that his irritation had quickly been replaced by concern. Something in the tone of her voice worried him. He was surprised to find that a part of him still cared.

"You're not hanging up," she said, relief in her voice. "Friends again?"

"I'm sorry it didn't work out," he said. "I admit I wasn't as supportive as I could have been, but there's nothing I can do to help you. I wish you luck."

It was Aimee's turn to be silent. "You really hurt me when you dumped me," she finally said. "I hated you for so long. You think I'm pathetic, don't you? You pity me. You're right. It was wrong for me to try to involve you in my problems. You don't understand; I don't think that you ever did. I'm on the threshold of an awakening and you're too close-minded to come along with me. It's been good talking with you again, Dennis."

She hung up before he could respond.

Pam was standing behind him. "She had the gall to call you again? That's one messed-up woman. Do we need to get an unlisted number?"

"I don't think so. I think it's over. Why does that worry me?"

"Because you're a masochist? She's as good excuse as any to get an answering machine."

She studied her medications for a minute, then closed the medicine cabinet. She didn't like taking the meds; they took away the dreams. The dreams were all she had. But they weren't dreams, were they? Not really. They were something more.

Her unemployment checks would end next week. She'd have to start looking for a job.

She took a beer from the refrigerator and went out to the porch. She pulled a chair next to the edge and sat with her feet propped up on the wooden guardrail.

A lone cicada wailed mournfully in the darkness. It was a cloudless, hot night. The moon was crystal sharp and detailed. She sipped her beer and remembered a recurring dream she'd had as a child: a gust of wind had picked her up and lifted her into the night sky. She recalled the sudden rush of terror, the cold wind pummeling her, sucking the breath from her body as she picked up speed, the moon growing larger, the world, her house and family falling farther beneath her. Then she would wake…

She put down the beer, stood, and reached for the moon.

The heat washed over her in waves. She could feel the wind buffeting her as she soared, senses magnified to an almost painful intensity. How could she have thought that what she was before was real and this was not? How could she have forgotten?

The distant ruins, closer now. Her shadow beneath her, racing across the rocky earth, joined by two other shadows like hers. She was not alone. Her ancient sisters had found her.

When Pam got home from work Dennis was already there, sitting at the kitchen table. She could tell from his expression that something was wrong.

"What is it? You sick?"

"Aimee's dead."

"Oh God."

"The police called me at work. Our number was written on a notepad by her phone. They questioned me about her."

She sat next to him. "What happened?"

"It seems that she jumped from her second story apartment porch late last night. One of the tenants found her in the morning. God, that flying shit. She really did it. I should have listened to her. She was trying to tell me and I didn't pick up on it. Really handled it good, didn't I?"

The night was stifling, the air heavy with humidity. An occasional ineffectual breeze carried the scent of summer flowers.

Pam and Dennis sat in their backyard, slaves to the god of lassitude. They were past the talking stage, content to gaze up at the summer constellations.

"What is that?" Pam muttered.

"What?"

"Look at the moon."

Three black shapes slowly flew across the face of the gibbous moon.

Dennis squinted. "So? They're birds. Maybe bats."

Pam sat up straight. "They're *huge!*"

Still silhouetted against the moon, the shapes changed direction toward Pam and Dennis.

Dennis stood. "Let's go inside."

"Kind of like big vultures," Pam said. "Do we have vultures this far north?"

The things dropped beneath the moon, disappearing into the darkness.

Dennis tugged Pam's arm. "C'mon."

"What's the rush?" she protested; she let him pull her to her feet.

They heard a distant sound carried on the breeze. Laughter. Women's laughter. Not a sound tempered by mirth, or pleasure. It had the tone of madness in it. And the predatory.

"Jesus, no," Dennis moaned, "it's impossible."

"Dennis, cut it out, you're freaking me," Pam said, her voice rising in panic.

Three massive dark shapes swooped low into the backyard, long wings extended, activating the security floodlights.

Pam screamed. One of the creatures broke away from the others and glided over to Dennis.

It wasn't until he saw its monstrous grinning face and recognized it that he started to scream.

MISSING

by Charles Ensminger

illustrated by Michael Ryan

This letter was sent to Dean R. Price of Davenburg Theological School. It came roughly a month after the disappearance of Gary Andover, a student at D.T.S., and was sent by Ian Hunter, also a student at D.T.S. Shortly after dropping off the letter, Ian Hunter also vanished. The current whereabouts of these two students are unknown. The text of the letter was not made public due to the fantastic nature of its contents. While having questioned students of the Theological School initially, investigators are still seeking Ian for questioning and suspect that he, contrary to his letter, was responsible for Gary Andover's disappearance.

Dean Price,

I write this letter to you in the hopes of explaining what I know to be the fate of Gary Andover. I know that from our past conversations you realized that I knew more than I was saying. I refrained from telling you this tale for the simple fact that it seemed to be as absurd and fanciful as claiming that the dog had eaten one's homework.

Yet so far as I can tell, this is what happened to Gary. I am writing this for your eyes only. If you think that this is a joke, so be it. But I also believe that you have a discerning mind, and you know I would not write something like this if I did not believe it to be true.

Gary and I met our first year here at seminary. As first year students, we had several classes together. And, both us being first year students, we bonded together loosely out of a sense of being overwhelmed and wanting to find someone to flounder through the lectures together.

Among my classmates, Gary was, by far, the most reserved. While I found that I had made several close friendships by the end of the first semester, it seemed that Gary had not. And, save for me, I don't think he talked to many people in the seminary at all.

But Gary and I seemed to form a special if not unique bond. For whatever reason, Gary opened up to me one afternoon following a lecture on the writings of the Desert Mystics. It seemed that their brand of Christianity alluded to something that Gary was interested in—the mystical planes of existence. Gary believed that the Desert Fathers' confrontations with demons and spirits from heaven and hell were quite literal and were but a glimpse into realities that we cannot fully fathom. I gathered this from our conversations, and I have to admit that the speculative ventures he and I would engage in were wonderful and (honestly) at times frightening.

Gary also believed that the Mystics partook of knowledge that the rest of humanity has quickly and quietly forgotten in an attempt to push it to the far recesses of our collective memory. Not far away enough not to be frightened in the cold and dark of the night, but far away enough where we cannot truly pinpoint what it is that frightens us.

In the course of our conversations, Gary and I proposed the idea (and I say we both did, since it came from our conversations, not posited by one of us alone) that the study of the Desert Mystics might provide some kind of clues or at least guidelines by which we could find more about these spiritual encounters. Yet, for all of our enthusiasm, classwork did not permit us the leisure time to study the Desert Fathers and, for my part, I let the issue slowly fade into a fond memory.

As we went our separate ways for the summer break, I lost touch with Gary—and I didn't think much about him. Most of my classmates fell out of touch over the summer, partly because we all believed that we would see each other again the following term. But when the second term began, I realized that, while I had enjoyed a relatively carefree summer, working in my home church as a youth director, Gary had been renewing his study of the Desert Mystics with zeal. From our early conversations that second year, I learned that he had read most of the mystics and had indeed found some quite obscure references to other, older works.

The Christian mystical writings, as he told me, became something of an enigma to him. He felt that they were too sanitized to be of any real use. All they contained were sayings and anecdotes about this hermit or that. They never dealt with anything concrete or tangible for the reader to use or utilize. It was almost as if the old scribes wrote on the periphery of the subject, protecting their knowledge from the idly curious, and

hoping to mollify readers with stories. They were only instructive in that they provided a basic philosophy, but little else. Gary was frustrated at the lack of information that these writings contained.

I had proposed to him that maybe that was the heart of it. Not so much the spiritual journeys and battles, but a purely theoretical philosophy of ecstatic experience that no one had actually undergone. But Gary disagreed. He disagreed because there was something else that he had discovered.

What troubled him the most was that it was in his study of Christian mystics that he began to find tales and sayings from *other* mystics—desert dwellers who were not persuaded by the Christian argument. Some, he said, were "Christian, but not only." Others were not Christian at all. But within these Hermetic and Gnostic writings, some only recently discovered in the Egyptian desert, he found what he and I had surmised might exist: a reference to the abilities to open doors to other realms.

It seemed that he had gone to great lengths to find some of these works. I gathered that they were not as easy to locate as I would have believed. Second-hand discussions of them were superficial to the point of uselessness, as if their authors did not really know the subject, or the relevant texts. Apparently he traveled to several different schools that had vast libraries, "far superior on the subject than ours," he would say. He had also made several contacts with other schools and had connected with online catalogues to find even more obscure works. Some had been published in small print runs and questionable translations by obscure Theosophical publishers with no academic credibility.

It was here that I chided him somewhat. I told him that with the internet, one could never be sure that what one read, or even saw, was real. I reminded him of the pranks some local college students had gotten in trouble over, with the convincing pictures they had put on the web. But he felt certain that the web pages he found were genuine. When I asked him how he was so sure, he responded, "Because of how they talked when we wrote back and forth. They knew more than I knew to ask." But that vague, general answer was all he would say. And that was really what disturbed me the most. It was as if he was either so preoccupied that he couldn't bear to take tangential conversations seriously, or he wouldn't answer because he didn't believe (and I know this sounds strange) I could really fathom what he had learned.

He did tell me that he had, in his research, learned of books that hinted at times before recorded history. If he hadn't been so serious in his tone, I would have joked about how if they were before recorded history, how would we have them to read? But there was something in his voice that I recognized as sincere. And it troubled me.

Some nights after we had come back from the break, he called me over to his room. There was something that he wanted to show me, and he wanted me to visit without anyone knowing I was there. "Watch your back," he said. And after I arrived (feeling foolish for checking that there was no one following me), he let me in with the suspicious glances of someone in a spy drama—I thought he was just overacting. But he was serious.

As you are probably aware, our rooms are not that large. Gary's was particularly small, in that he had managed to get a prized private room in the seminary dorm, a floor above mine (which added to the absurdity of his worrying about me being followed. We lived in the same building!). But the room was as Spartan as a monastic cell. No pictures, no knick-knacks, none of the trivialities that we all seem to accumulate so quickly. Rather, there was just a computer, a television with a DVD/VHS player, a small tape recorder, and neatly shelved books.

Yet sitting on the corner of his desk was what appeared to be a fragile, antique volume. It was no more than a half-inch thick, withered and weathered as if it had survived into the modern era by sheer willpower. It was like one of those books that the library stores in small boxes, that have to be unfolded to open and retrieve the book. Even then, it was worn beyond belief.

It was this book that he wanted me to see. I knew it from the moment I walked into his room, and even before he said anything. The book was something important. He motioned to the desk and gestured at the chair. He sat on the edge of his bed and looked at me with the eyes of someone who has found buried treasure.

"I realize that I have been acting rather strange as of late. And I owe you an apology. You see, the ideas we talked about last year have nearly driven me mad, trying to prove them. I believed that we were on to something, and I realized that you might believe it, but you weren't as interested in the idea as I was. I don't mean any disrespect in saying that. It's just that my nature is stirred by things that don't move most people. I am an outcast in most circles, and yet you managed to be more open to me than anyone else I have met. Yet even you aren't like me."

I protested a little. I didn't think we were alike, but I assured him that our ideas were indeed similar. But he held up his hand.

"Don't be offended. You are truly my only good friend. And I wanted to share something with you. I think I am on to something, and, if so, you are the only person that would even remotely understand what it is I am after. You may not see me much anymore. But, if I can, before I go, I will visit with you one more time. You deserve to know the truth about our ideas."

"Where are you going?" I asked, thinking that he was possibly considering leaving school.

"You know where I am going, if you really think about it. But it seems too hard to conceive of right now. Wait until the early hours of the morning and think on it. Then *nothing* seems preposterous. But for now, I want to tell you a few things."

"Does this book have something to do with it?" I asked.

He seemed to suddenly come alive with a ferocity and fervor that I had never seen in him.

"Yes! Yes it does! That book is something I never thought I would ever hold in my hands, let alone be able to take possession of!"

"This didn't come from the library?"

"No. Not this one. I found it in a library at the… well, at a different school. It wasn't properly shelved. And when I looked at it, I realized that it wasn't properly cataloged either. So I smuggled it out."

"You stole it?" I asked, completely shocked.

"Yes. Well, liberated it. It was left to decay. But it is richness beyond that of any imagination. It is a peal of great price, cast before swine. It was waiting for me, and it is rightfully mine. This text is *thousands* of years old. What I have here is a Greek translation, though I have no idea what the original language might have been." His face was practically beaming, unhealthily flushed, as it seemed to me, especially given his usual bookworm pallor.

"The text is called 'The Gospel of the Twins,' though I think it was originally called something else. Possibly 'The Message of the Revealers' or some such."

He had me there. I had never heard of "The Gospel of the Twins" or "The Message of the Revealers," and I considered myself pretty well read in non-canonical literature. But I would come to find out that there was research on this text. In fact, I would learn more and more about this gospel over the coming weeks. It seems that the Gospel of the Twins belongs to a larger category of writings that have never been adequately cataloged. While they sound much like the proclamation literature known as gospels, they have little to do with the Christian canon. At least, that is what I believe about them. They are allegedly the stories and collected teachings of

beings known as Kara and Adem, characters I had never heard of prior to my conversations with Gary.

But Gary insisted that these stories and sayings went back to the time before recorded history. As Gary would finally say, "The time before Atlantis was great, when other societies existed that could have rivaled our own." So it seems that these documents tell of a world that existed and vanished long before Plato. Yet Gary went on to claim that these works themselves came from cultures that existed before Noah! The Nephilim mentioned in Genesis 6 are the last remnants of that society. Destroyed, as it were, by God. Now, as I'm sure you know, the beginning of the Flood story in Genesis, chapter six is usually given short shrift in Bible classes, when not ignored completely. Verses one through four contain odd details that seem to be the tip of some other iceberg, not originally part of the Noah story. That stuff about ancient sons of God mating with human females. Yet in some respects it is an explanation as to why the flood occurs at all. As if someone had polluted God's creation so badly, he had to trash it and start over again. I haven't really studied up on it, but Gary was convinced that this, like so many other puzzles, pointed back to a time that we know next to nothing about.

I realize, Dean, that this letter is spinning wildly out of control. But the story—the events of those last days with Gary—did just that.

Gary believed that this Gospel of the Twins was further evidence that the idea he and I had come up with was true. He had found that the ancient desert writers and mystics had been in touch (and according to him) traveled to other realities and universes. I pointed out that he was going way beyond anything we had surmised from the Desert Fathers, Gary had uncovered writings over that summer told much more. He had them all in a file tucked away in a locked cabinet in his room's closet. Pages and pages of photocopies and notes. And though I was intrigued by their content, I was beginning to fear for Gary's sanity. His obsession with them was frightening.

One morning before classes, he called me again to his room. It was a Thursday, and that morning was quite

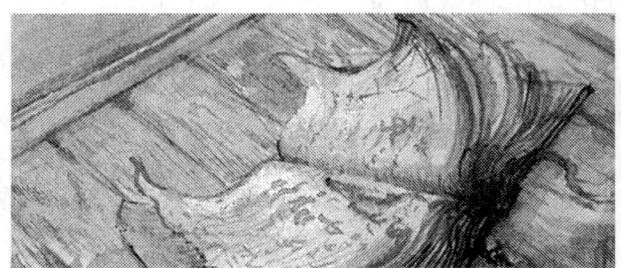

clear. He opened the door only far enough for half of his face to be visible to me.

"Are you going to chapel today?" he asked in a hushed voice.

"Yes. I thought I would," I replied.

"I need something. But I dare not leave this room unattended. The wall is getting thinner and thinner. And who knows what would happen if someone else entered before all was set!"

"What do you mean? What's getting thinner? Are you all right? Is there some kind of danger?"

"No. No, no. Not danger. More like fire. Fire is only dangerous if abused or mishandled. But I do need your help."

"What, then?" I was quite concerned.

And then in a hushed tone, he said, "Bring back some of the elements for me."

"You want me to bring you communion?" I felt a wave of relief. Perhaps he feared getting out, but if all he wanted was for someone to bring him communion, I could easily do that. In fact, I had more than once taken communion from church to elderly shut-ins.

"Yes, yes. I can do that. Is that all?"

"Bring extra." And with that, he closed the door.

That afternoon following the chapel service, I asked Dr. Wallage if I could have some of the elements for a few of my friends in the college who couldn't make it to chapel. He obliged me. He wouldn't have, had he known what I was going to do with them, nor would I have asked if I had known.

I returned to the dorm, now quite empty since most everyone was at lunch. I knocked on Gary's door. For a moment, I thought no one was going to answer, that he had decided to go out after all. Then I heard what sounded like a low electric hum—like you might hear at the back of a refrigerator. I put my ear close to the door. I heard a shuffling, as if someone was clearing papers or getting up off the floor. And then the door opened.

Gary yanked me inside, almost like a slapstick comedy scene, shutting the door quickly behind me. The room had a strange purplish tint to it. Like sunlight through a violet curtain. But there was no sunlight coming through that window. The light was coming from the window, but the view on the other side was nothing that I have ever seen on this earth. And from the other side, from some indistinguishable distance, I could hear a chanting like that of Buddhist monks holding a low, resonant note. It was everywhere, hanging like a sonic mist, but not loud. Loud enough to be heard through the door, but not much further away than that.

Gary looked at me. "The elements?" He held out his hands.

I handed him the elements—the wine was in a small plastic container. There was enough for four, maybe five, small communion cups. And there were four pieces of the bread.

"This is still sacred?"

"I suppose so. It was consecrated"

"Good. You took communion, I suppose?"

"Of course."

"Then forgive me if I only offer you one more piece and take the other three for myself."

"Why?"

"I don't know how much fortitude they will provide, but I believe that communion was part of the key."

I had started to say something, but he held up his hand.

"Let me explain quickly. You see, the mystics would indeed open doors to other planes. Sometimes things would rush out, and sometimes they would rush in. The only way they felt they could survive whatever came out, or the only way they could survive crossing over, was to be fortified through communion. Hundreds of centuries ago, though, it wasn't a Christian ceremony. But the idea was the same. By eating the body and drinking the blood of God, one was empowered to *move* like a god. If only for a short while—a few hours, possibly a day, maybe a few days.

"The mystics would fast for days in preparation. Then they would practice eating. Just a few pieces of bread and a small drink of juice or wine. Then they would fast again and measure the time before they excreted what they had eaten. They could then measure the time they would have before the effects of the food wore off. Then, when they had a good feel for time, they would take communion, or some type of ritual meal and, being empowered by God, they would venture forth or see if something would come through.

"The Gospel of the Twins mentions briefly that when Adem returned to his realm, people could see through to where he was, but no one could follow. The mystics figured out that they could go through, but just for a while. Now I have the opportunity to go through, too."

"You have got to be kidding me! Where are you going? What the hell is that in your window? Some sort of black light display? And what makes you think it will take you anywhere at all? This is absurd!"

"The window is my portal. A bit lame, metaphorically speaking, but it works. And the portal was the easy part. I found a liturgy of summoning in the Third Letter of Didymus the Simonian. The hard part was finding how to get through safely. I've been spending weeks trying to determine how long I could go. I think I can hold on, over on that side, for just about two days. That's enough for a trial run. The extra communion elements are if I need more fortification once I cross over."

"And for me? I don't plan on going over!"

"Of course not. You aren't prepared to go. But I need you here. You have to be my anchor. You might have to pull me through. I don't know. But if you do, you need to eat the communion elements before you reach across to me. I need you to sit here and wait."

"For *two days*?"

"Perhaps. But I need you! You are the only person alive who has any idea what I am trying to do. You are the only one who could possibly understand. Once I cross this threshold, you must lock the door to this room and wait. No one must come in. You have to help me!"

I have to admit, I hated being put on the spot like that. And after we exchanged arguments, I caved in. He took the wafers and wine and shook my hand. Then he stepped into the glowing portal and vanished right in front of me! For a brief moment, I could almost make him out walking beyond the window—where there was nothing but air on any given day!

I turned and locked the door and sat at the desk, staring in awe at what had just happened. Gary had walked out of the very world! I hadn't even begun to prepare myself for the two day vigil when all at once Gary reemerged.

"Good Lord! Gary! Are you all right?"

His eyes were wide. He looked as if he were in shock.

"I can't believe it! Three whole days! In the fields of the Lands Above the Mountains! I can't believe it!"

He went on and on like that for some time. Apparently he was convinced he had managed to stay on the other side for three days, where here it had only been three to five minutes. He told me in choppy sequence of walking into a beautiful land and wandering through a field that, according to some of the texts he had read, floated above some unknown mountain range. He said that he could see a staircase that reached even higher heavenward and could see cities below in the mountains. He had slept under alien skies and alien stars but had little time to venture either up to the unknown or to find some passage to the city below.

And then he collapsed into a dead sleep. I stayed with him until he awoke. He then asked if I could excuse him, as he had some writing to do.

We had other conversations later, Dean Price. I must say that what he said he saw was unbelievable. Just out of the question. Captivating, though. The possibility was wondrous. And I have to admit that I began to wish that

I had also ventured there. Yet I digress.

Only one thing remains to tell you. And that was of the day he did not return.

Only a week after the events I have just described, Gary once again opened a portal. Again, he asked for me to bring him communion elements. More than last time, if possible. And, like the Thursday prior, it was a beautiful morning.

As I headed back to the dorm that day, I noticed that the beautiful morning was turning into a menacing afternoon. The sky was a ferocious black behind the dorm, and it seemed to be headed towards the heart of campus with a tremendous wind. Perhaps you remember it? It was the day that the power went out for several hours. That night there would be a phone message that said there was some kind of "hiccup" in the power grid. I know better, and soon you will, too.

As last time, I brought Gary the communion elements. And, as before, he headed into the portal. But this portal was not the violet glowing one I had seen before. Rather it was a violent orange, and the chanting sounded unharmonious and disconcerting. And as before, I told Gary I would sit vigil.

Gary stepped forward through the window and at once emitted a shriek that sounded as if he were being torn to pieces. I could see nothing, but then Gary's hands emerged, and I heard his voice calling for help. I jumped towards the window and grabbed his hands. With my face that close, I could see black eyes behind Gary looking at me. I pulled hard, and Gary came through. But not all of him. His legs were gone from the knee down. His terrible wounds, though, were cauterized. Cut off with extreme heat. What could do that, I do not know. But the wounds were jagged around the edges, as if the rest had been eaten off.

Grabbing at some paper, Gary, somehow still coherent, read and then laughed, blowing blood out his nose as he did. He then rolled on his back, closed his eyes and began to chant.

I stepped out of the room for only a minute. I thought

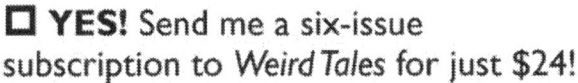

Gary needed water. I was also going to call 911 when I got back. But when I re-entered the room, Gary was pulling himself towards the portal again. I tried to stop him, but he actually managed to fight me off.

"I know what went wrong. Now let me go. If I have to die, let me die in the fields of the Lands Above the Mountains!"

It was then that I noticed that the portal had changed from that wicked orange to the more placid violet. I suppose that the skies had changed by then, too. You see, what I would find out in the ensuing days was that Gary had made a mistake in the summoning of the portal. The fragment of paper that he had grasped when he came back through was the piece of the work known as the Third Letter of Didymus the Simonian. I would later find out that this work was considered vile magic. This Didymus was apparently one of the few people who knew of the magic doors that could lead to other places. He wrote a letter describing them and how to make them. The Second Letter was one of the documents that Gary had photocopied from some arcane library I never would find. But the so-called Third Letter, which was something of a corruption of the Second, was *also* something he had copied.

The Third Letter was a corruption, as I have said, and considered particularly heinous. That's because whoever wrote it left out particular elements of spells and incantations so that the reader would inevitably cause himself great harm, even death. Gary had read the corrupted version by accident and opened a portal to as close to hell as I ever want to see. He had come through and realized his mistake. Apparently, while I was out of the room, he issued the proper incantation and opened the "right" portal. He crawled through and, after about thirty minutes, the portal closed. I suppose that was about a month on his side.

I have never laid eyes upon Gary again. I still have most of his records and writings, though I have little desire to release them to you, or to anyone else. I write this to let you know what took place. Yet you will not be able to find me to talk about it. By the time you read this, I will be long gone. But I will quote you one passage that the Second Letter has that the Third does not. If I had known it then, I could have saved him.

"And upon opening the gates of the gods, look you closely at the portents in the skies. Should the darkness rise from the West, then, amen I say, walk not into the gates, for the dark omens in the skies point to despair for those who would pass through the gate of the furnace. For therein lie The Untouched Ones, sprung from the burning Abyss. Rather, I say, seek for the purple hues of evening, knowing that the Lands Above the Mountains are nigh." — Ian Hunter

CHILLED RED

She takes her reds chilled —
torn raw from the cellar,
permitted no breath,
no life-giving warmth.

Not for her Syrah spice
or a blossoming Burgundy
bold on her tongue
like a ribald French kiss.

Enophile friends despair,
dare to tempt her
with well-aired balloons
wafting scent of the grape.

She wants none of theirs,
prefers her own bottles
kept iced on the sly,
poured quick & sipped quicker.

The risk is too present
for gourmet pretensions:
let them think harshly
of her, & survive.

She takes her reds chilled,
lest she waken a craving
for what she'd far rather
be drinking tonight.

— Ann K. Schwader

 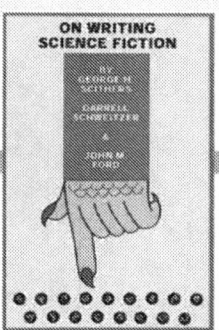 

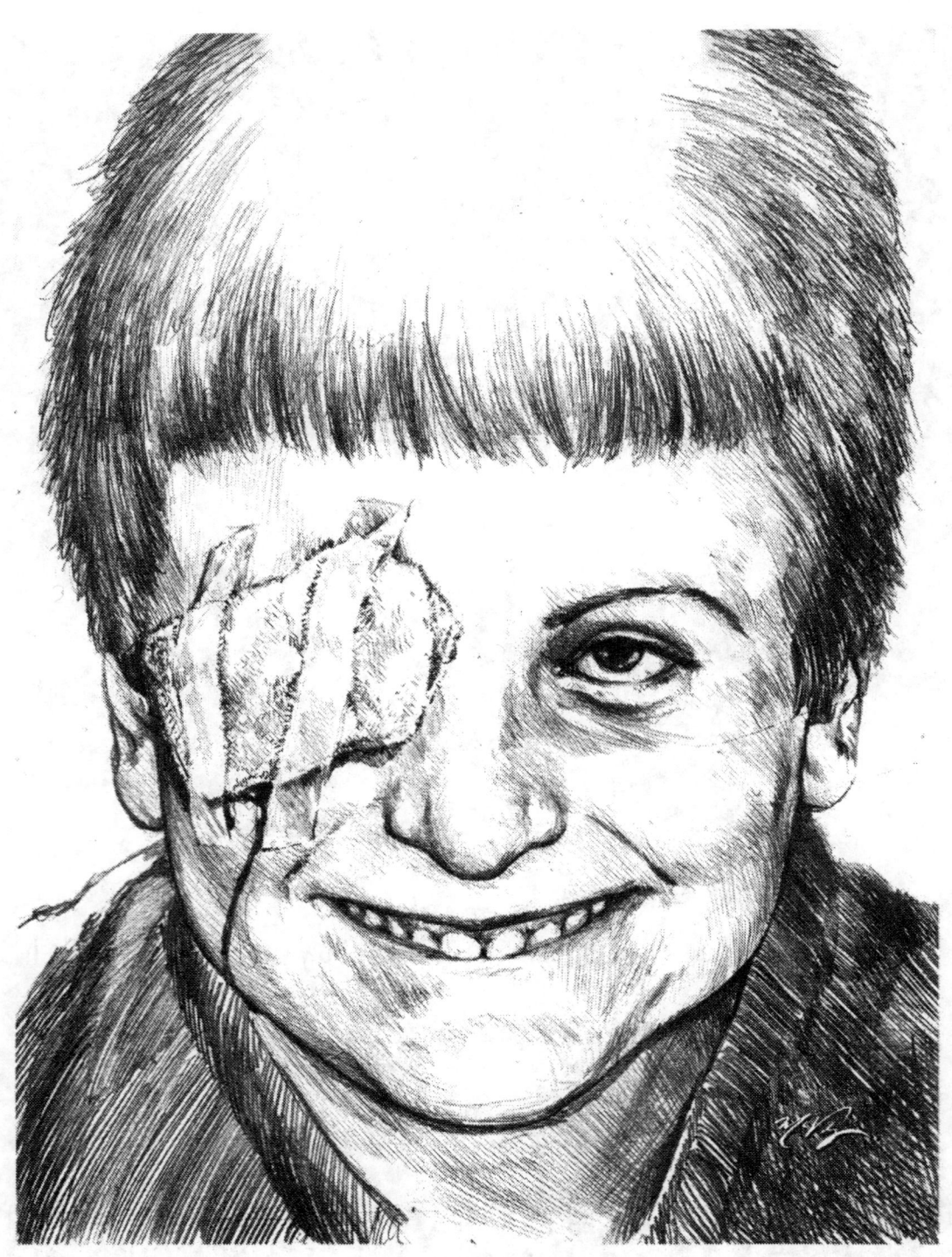

www.ingramcontent.com/pod-product-compliance
Lightning Source LLC
Chambersburg PA
CBHW080811120626
46556CB00009B/3290